ECO-WORRIERS

Saving
the Bacon

Kathryn Lamb lives in Dorset with her children.
As well as writing books, she draws cartoons for
Private Eye, *The Oldie*, *The Spectator* and
The Blackmore Vale Magazine.

Also by Kathryn Lamb:

Eco-Worriers: *Penguin Problems*
Eco-Worriers: *Tree Trouble*
Best Mates Forever: *Vices and Virtues*
Is Anyone's Family As Mad As Mine?

ECO-WORRIERS

Saving the Bacon

Kathryn Lamb

Piccadilly Press • London

For Safia, Jasper, Lexus, Lunah and Juliette

First published in Great Britain in 2008
by Piccadilly Press Ltd,
5 Castle Road, London NW1 8PR
www.piccadillypress.co.uk

Text copyright © Kathryn Lamb, 2008

A catalogue record for this book is available from the British Library

ISBN: 978 1 85340 990 5 (trade paperback)

1 3 5 7 9 10 8 6 4 2

Printed and bound in Great Britain by CPI Bookmarque, Croydon
Cover design by Simon Davis
Cover illustration by Sue Hellard

Chapter One

'*Rubbish!*' *Evie exclaims* in disgust. 'There's rubbish everywhere!'

Looking around the school courtyard, I see that she is right. A chilly November wind has blown rubbish from the overflowing bin and scattered it around. Little eddies of empty crisp packets, cereal bar wrappers and scrumpled bits of paper are whirling around, and a few careless people have obviously been dropping empty drinks cartons, banana skins, apple cores and plastic bottles on the ground, probably because the bin was full.

'Honestly! Couldn't they be bothered to take them to the recycling bins?' Evie asks, bending down to pick up two empty plastic bottles. 'Lazy pigs!'

I help Evie by scooping up a few more bottles and a couple of cartons which I stuff into the side pocket of my schoolbag until I can get to the recycling bins. 'Pigs aren't lazy,' I comment. 'They're really intelligent.'

'Liam's supposed to be intelligent,' Evie replies. 'But he's also lazy. He's always sprawled on the sofa, watching TV. He's a lazy pig.'

'Stop saying that! Pigs don't have sofas – or TVs. Pig are cool. I like pigs. At least they don't drop litter everywhere.'

'True.' One of the bottles which Evie has stuffed in the pocket of her blazer falls to the ground and rolls in front of Miss Peabody, the tiny birdlike geography teacher, who is just crossing the courtyard.

'Pick that up at once, Evie!' she twitters. 'I would have expected better of you than to drop litter!'

'But . . . but . . . but . . .' Evie protests.

Miss Peabody doesn't wait to listen, and scuttles away just as the bell rings for the end of break and the start of afternoon lessons.

The day does not improve. Evie and I usually enjoy lessons with Mr Woodsage, the friendliest and most eco-minded of the teachers at Shrubberylands Comprehensive. He is back to teaching after breaking both legs when he fell off his roof while checking his wind turbine, and he is still on crutches.

'Some of you may be distressed by the film we are about to watch,' he says, as the blinds in the room are pulled down, and everyone's eyes are drawn to the large screen.

This proves to be an understatement. We are watching some sort of horror film about chickens. There is a huge dusty shed crammed with birds, almost unrecognisable as chickens as they have lost most of their feathers, and a few of them are lying dead on the floor while the others stagger and jostle around them. The commentary tells us that these are intensively-farmed standard chickens being reared for slaughter, and there are up to forty thousand of them in the shed, which has no natural daylight. The lights are left on for twenty-three hours a day to make the chickens feed continuously until they get so fat that their legs can no longer support them. Many of them have hock burns on their legs from living in their own dirt, and their short, unhappy lives come to an end at only thirty-nine days, when they are taken away for slaughter, to be sold cheaply in supermarkets.

'This is so awful!' I whisper to Evie, tears in my eyes. 'Chickens should be allowed to fly around, wild and free, like other birds.' I am passionate about birds – bird-watching is one of my hobbies.

'I don't think chickens fly much,' says Evie. 'But I know what you mean. Those conditions are awful and something should be done.' Her bottom lip trembles and she puts her arm around my shoulders.

Mr Woodsage stops the film and switches on the lights. Most of the girls are crying, including Evie and me, and many of the boys are white-faced, with shocked expressions on their faces.

'It makes you think twice about your chicken nuggets and chicken burgers, doesn't it?' says Mr Woodsage in a slightly choked voice, taking off his little round glasses, which have misted up, and giving them a wipe. He holds up a sheet of A4 paper. 'You see this sheet of paper?' he asks. 'This is all the space that one of those chickens has to live its entire life in. That particular chicken shed, which you saw in the film, belongs to Reginald Rooster of Reginald Rooster's Farmfresh Foods, which is a huge company some of you may be familiar with.'

Evie makes a disgusted noise. 'Liam's always scoffing Reginald Rooster rubbish!' she exclaims. 'Micronuggets – those are his favourite. Yuck!'

'But, sir, why doesn't someone stop it?' I call out. 'It's awful to keep chickens like that! It's cruel! It's wrong!'

The whole class joins in the chorus of outrage and disapproval, until Mr Woodsage calls for quiet.

'Fortunately people are a lot more aware of the problem now,' he says. 'And you can go online to sign e-petitions to improve the welfare of chickens, pigs and other farm animals. So there is a move to stop the

4

cruelty and improve the chickens' lives. But as long as there is a demand for cheap chicken, the terrible things that you saw in the film may continue.'

Mr Woodsage then shows us the second part of the film, which is about happy chickens living in much better conditions. I expect he is showing us the happy chicken film so that we don't become seriously depressed – the school probably can't afford counselling for so many traumatised students.

The happy chicken film is encouraging. The free-range chickens live in a shed with access to outside and what the commentary refers to as plenty of 'environmental enrichment' including footballs, CDs on strings to peck at, ladders and bales of straw to perch on, hanging bundles of maize and a lot more space to live in, although their barn is still fairly crowded. The organic chickens fare even better, with pesticide-free food as well as access to an outdoor grassed area where they can forage and dust-bathe. They look completely different from the pathetic, featherless, intensively-farmed birds – the free-range ones have sleek brown feathers and a spring in their step.

'All chickens should live like that,' says Evie firmly, when the film has ended.

Mr Woodsage nods agreement and continues. 'These fortunate organic chickens are slower-growing, get slaughtered at eighty days instead of forty, and cost at least twice as much per bird in the supermarket. They are also free from the antibiotics which are pumped into the intensively-farmed ones to stop infections from spreading in cramped conditions, and which inevitably get into the food chain when the chickens are slaughtered and eaten.'

Evie looks at him rather fiercely. 'If we all turned vegetarian, they wouldn't need to get slaughtered at all,' she says.

'What a horrible day!' Evie exclaims, as we run to her house to get out of a sudden ice-cold shower of rain. We hang our wet coats and bags in the hall, and race upstairs to her room.

'You left your lights on all day,' I observe. 'That's a black mark on your eco-chart.'

'I told you it was a horrible day,' Evie grumbles. 'I get accused of being a litterbug when I'm only trying to help, then we have to watch a gruesome chicken film, and now I'm burning holes in the ozone layer. So much for reducing my carbon footprint to become as dainty as possible. That does it! I'm turning vegetarian.'

'I thought you were already vegetarian.'

'I was – I mean, I am – and then I had a sausage. And it was so nice that I had another one. It was a momentary lapse.'

'Was that chicken sandwich in the canteen another

momentary lapse?' I inquire.

'NO! DO NOT TALK TO ME ABOUT CHICKEN! I feel like a murderer! I will never *ever* eat chicken again after that film! Or any other kind of meat. I feel *sick*. Vegetarianism is the *only* option. Don't you agree?'

'Er . . .'

'LOLA?!'

'I mean, of course.' I am not sure about this. I hate the idea of chickens suffering and I don't want to eat any Reginald Rooster stuff, but I'm not sure whether I want to turn vegetarian . . .

'So you'll be a vegetarian, too? Promise?'

'Yeees. Absolutely.' Evie is so fired up that I don't want to upset her by refusing to become a vegetarian. Maybe I *can* do it. 'I certainly wouldn't eat any of Reginald Rooster's products – that was revolting. I'm going to have nightmares about those poor chickens.'

Evie shakes her head. 'It's so wrong,' she says. 'I'm going to stop Mum from buying any more Reginald Rooster rubbish. Come on!'

We go downstairs to the kitchen, where Evie's mum is peeling potatoes and Liam is preparing himself a snack. To my horror, I see that he is squeezing Reginald Rooster's Hot 'n' Spicy Chicken Spread from a tube on to a thick slice of white bread. The chicken spread is a strange off-pink colour.

Evie takes one look at what he is doing and her face turns a shade of off-green. She gags loudly and runs from the kitchen. We hear her retching in the downstairs loo.

'Oh dear – what's wrong?' says her mum, looking worried.

'Er . . . I think it's Liam,' I stammer, blushing.

Liam gives me a mock-offended look from behind his long dark fringe, which flops across his face. 'OK, so I'm not her favourite brother. But I am her only brother. And I'm the one who's teaching her to play the guitar. So she's going to have to get over it and try not to throw up every time she sees me. But I hope she's OK.' He sits down at the kitchen table and tucks into his chicken spread sandwich.

Evie reappears, looking pale beneath her fringe – she has had a fringe since last week when she had her hair cut and layered, and I think the new style suits her. Between us we manage to convince her anxious mum that Evie is not ill and then we explain about the chicken film. Evie tells her mum that she is now even more of a vegetarian than she was before and that I have said that I will become one as well, and then she tells Liam that he must stop eating Reginald Rooster products and asks her mum to stop buying them. She says that we must all do everything we can to promote the welfare of chickens and other farm animals. Then she pauses for breath.

Liam looks at us thoughtfully. His dark brown eyes always send my insides on a rollercoaster ride! Then he takes another bite of his sandwich. 'I can't stand all this green guilt-tripping,' he says thickly, mid-munch. 'It's not going to save a chicken's life if I stop eating this sandwich.'

'But it will!' Evie insists. 'If the demand for cheap chicken goes down, and people stop buying bargain basement birds by the bucket-load, then those horrible intensive chicken farms will close down.' She tries to explain the difference between free-range chickens and organic ones, and gets confused about which of them go outside. 'Free-range sounds as if they *ought* to roam around freely, doesn't it? But I think it's the organic ones. Oh, I don't know!'

'It's a terrible thing not to know your chickens,' Liam remarks, leaning back in his chair and burping loudly. 'But there's an easy way to tell – the organic ones have four legs instead of two. Or is it the free-range ones?' He burps loudly again.

'Liam!' Evie's mum exclaims reprovingly.

'The trouble is, I just don't have strong feelings about chickens,' says Liam. 'You can't take a chicken for a walk. They don't sit on your lap and purr.'

'They play football,' I interject. Liam ignores me. OK. He thinks I'm mad. Now I'm blushing again.

'I'll ask Mr Woodsage if I can bring that film home to show you,' Evie insists stubbornly. 'Then you'll change your mind.'

'I suppose,' I begin tentatively, trying to sound sane and sensible after my footballing-chickens remark, 'I suppose that it's better to buy happy, healthy locally-produced chickens rather than intensively-farmed ones which might have to be driven or even flown long distances to reach your plate. You'd be cutting down on food miles and supporting your local community.'

'And what about the chicken farmers left scratching in the dirt by your Buy Local campaign?' Liam retorts, staring at me challengingly. 'And besides, in order to produce enough free-range chickens to feed everyone, the whole country would be overrun by chickens. We'd all be tripping over them! The foxes wouldn't mind – they'd all get fat! Foxes take a lot of free-range chickens. Being free-range isn't all fun and frolics. Don't you know anything?'

My blush-ometer swings to maximum – red alert! Red alert! I wish I'd kept my mouth shut.

'Leave Lola alone!' says Evie defensively, putting her arm round my shoulders.

She turns to her mum. 'Mum – you won't buy any more cheap chicken, will you?'

Liam chuckles. 'Chicken going cheap! Cheep cheep!'

Evie rounds on him. 'Idiot!' she snarls.

'And you're a green meanie who puts the "mental" into environmental!' Liam retorts.

'Oh – stop it! Both of you!' exclaims their mum in exasperation. 'I understand what you're saying, love,' she says, soothingly. 'But organic chicken is very expensive. I could get a free-range chicken occasionally and I'll certainly try to avoid getting Reginald Rooster products. If you're serious about being a vegetarian this time' – Evie nods vigorously – 'there are plenty of really nice vegetarian recipes we can try, if you like. You've always enjoyed my vegetarian lasagne, haven't you?'

'Thanks, Mum!' Evie gives her mum a hug.

'No problem,' says Liam, pushing his chair back, getting up and stretching. 'I can buy meat for myself if I want to, now I've got a job. Talking of which, I'd better go and get ready.'

'What's Liam doing?' I whisper to Evie after he has gone.

'Driving me round the bend, as usual,' she replies.

'No – I mean, he's got a job?'

'Oh, he's a waiter at Luigi's.'

Luigi's is a café which serves bistro-style food and is very popular with the Sixth-Formers as it is one of the few trendy places in the neighbourhood. Luigi is the brother of our friend Meltonio. Meltonip sells eco-friendly ice-cream from an eco-friendly ice-cream van, although not usually in the winter months, so he then works at his brother's café.

I decide Liam probably looks good in a waiter's uniform, but I decide not to confide this thought to Evie.

Back home I am getting ready for bed, a jumble of tired thoughts cluttering my brain, prominent among which is an image of a dead, featherless chicken being trampled by other chickens. I try to replace it with an image of Liam in a smart waiter's uniform, complete with black bow tie . . .

Eco-info

The annual consumption of eggs in the UK would stretch fifteen times round the world. There will be a ban on battery farming by 2012 - battery hens are kept in cramped conditions, six to a cage, whereas free-range hens are free to roam. Look for the words 'free-range' or the RSPCA Freedom Food Mark on supermarket chickens; this means they will have lived happy, healthy lives.

Chapter Two

'So *what did* you dream about last night, Lola?' Evie inquires, breathlessly. We are jogging to school – or, at least, I am jogging, as part of my training to try out for the next Olympics, and Evie is panting alongside me as she struggles to keep up. A cold wind is blowing the last leaves from the trees. 'I didn't sleep much,' she continues. 'I couldn't stop thinking about those poor chickens. And then I dreamed about them.'

I try to recall a vivid dream, which I know I had, although the details are becoming hazy. I dreamed about Liam, dressed as a waiter . . . There was a fire at the café and suddenly Liam was dressed as a fireman . . . and then I was running down Frog Street pursued by a giant frog . . . As dreams go, it was one of my weirder ones, and it had absolutely nothing to do with chickens. I decide not to tell Evie about it.

'I couldn't sleep,' I say. This is true – I lay awake for ages, worrying about the promise which Evie extracted from me to become a vegetarian. I have tried vegetarianism before, on a part-time basis, but I found it difficult to stick to because I love sausages . . . and chicken drumsticks . . .

'You're drooling,' Evie remarks. 'Why?'

'I'm not drooling!' I retort indignantly, wiping my mouth on my sleeve. Perhaps if I keep an image of one of Reginald Rooster's intensively-reared chickens staggering around in my mind, it will inspire me to stick to being a vegetarian.

'We need to reform the eating habits of the entire school!' Evie announces suddenly.

Oh no. Why does she always have to take things too far? I'm going to have enough trouble reforming my own eating habits.

'Everyone's bingeing on junk and additives,' Evie continues, warming to her theme. 'And then there's the packaging problem. All these snacks are wrapped in plastic – it's really bad for the environment. Look at that!'

'What?'

Evie points to a nearby tree where a plastic bag, blown by the wind, has been caught in the bare branches and is now flapping sadly like a crumpled and grubby flag.

'Literally billions of plastic bags get thrown away every single day – it's plastic pollution. There's even a great vortex of them swirling around in the Pacific Ocean, and turtles think that they are jellyfish and choke to death on them. It's awful! We must persuade people to cut down on packaging and stop using plastic bags! Oh – for goodness' sake!'

Evie's exclamation is directed at the tall, languid figure of Amelia Plunkett slowly drifting through the school gates ahead of us, her long blond hair lifting in the breeze. She is accompanied by her best friend, Jemima, and a gaggle of giggling wannabe Amelias, known to us as the So Cool Girls. Amelia is swinging a bright pink plastic bag in one hand and swigging the last drops from a plastic bottle of water in the other. Then she tosses the bottle on to the ground behind her and leaves it there. This is what causes Evie to exclaim.

'You dropped this, Amelia!' Evie shouts, retrieving the bottle and catching up with her. I follow along to lend Evie my support.

'So?' says Amelia witheringly, looking down her long thin nose at us. 'It's my bottle – I can do what I like with it. By the way, your hair's gone all frizzy,' she adds, staring at Evie's hair. 'I think that fringe is a mistake. Fringes are sooo yesterday . . .'

'Leave Evie alone!' I snap back, while Evie fumes alongside me and fires a look-to-kill straight at

Amelia. 'And why don't you recycle your empty bottle?' I suggest. 'Or better still, you can refill it with tap water so you don't need to buy another bottle.'

'Eurgh! Tap water!' Amelia spits in disgust. 'Tap water's full of hormones and bacteria swimming around! Don't you know that?'

'No it isn't!' I exclaim. 'Tap water's fine! It's cheap and it's good for you to drink lots of water. What's the point of shipping H_2O a gazillion ungreen miles around the world when you live in a home blessed with sanitary tap water?'

Amelia pulls a disgusted face.

'Why are you carrying a plastic bag, Amelia?' Evie demands, challengingly. 'Plastic bags are plastic pollution.'

'I don't know what you two sad freaks are on about,' says Amelia dismissively. 'This bag is from a designer clothes shop in Milan. My mum brought it back from a shopping holiday – this is a real designer plastic bag.'

The So Cool Girls crowd around going 'ooh' and 'aah' and admiring the bag. I pull Evie away before her exasperation with Amelia boils over.

'Who does she think she is?' Evie exclaims. 'Just because she's rich and has amazing hair!'

'But you've got amazing hair, too, Evie!' I point out. '*And* you care about the planet!'

Evie is still flushed red with anger and her curls are

fiery. 'This cold damp weather makes my hair go frizzy!' she complains. 'Whereas Amelia's hair is dead straight.'

This is true; the tight curls of Evie's recently acquired fringe have pouffed up and are standing out from her forehead. But I still think her new, choppy style suits her.

'Why don't we target some people who are a little less brain dead?' I suggest, steering the conversation away from Amelia and hair, just as two very overweight boys barge past us, stuffing their faces with chocolate bars and dropping the wrappers on the ground. They are Jamie and Oliver, and they are junk food addicts.

'Pick those wrappers up and put them in the bin!' Evie shouts angrily. Jamie and Oliver ignore her. 'Why don't you eat fruit instead?' she yells at them.

Jamie stops and looks back at her over his shoulder. He looks genuinely scared, as if she has threatened him with something awful. Then he wobbles away after the retreating figure of Oliver.

Evie sighs. 'Where are the teachers when you want them?' she asks. 'They're supposed to hand out instant detentions to anyone dropping litter. It makes me so angry! I'm going to have a real go at the next person I see stuffing their face with junk and throwing the rubbish on the floor! I'm going to take whoever it is by the scruff of the neck and march them round to the recycling bins.'

I nudge Evie with my elbow. 'Here comes someone,' I whisper.

It is Ben from Year Ten. He is eating a bag of crisps. Then he crumples up the empty packet and throws it at an overflowing litter bin. It misses, and joins the other bags and wrappers which are beginning, once again, to blow around the chilly courtyard.

'Go on, then!' I urge Evie. 'Have a go at him!' But Evie has clammed up completely. I have noticed that she tends to become tongue-tied and totally un-Evie-like whenever Ben from Year Ten is around.

She clears her throat nervously. 'Hi, Ben!' she says, in a flirty, girlie voice.

'Right,' I say, when Ben has passed by (he didn't seem to notice us at all). 'You certainly sorted *him* out. You had a real go at him. You —'

'Lola . . .'

'Yes?'

'Shut up. It's bad enough that he saw me looking like a bright red dandelion with my frizzed-up hair! Am I blushing, Lola?'

Evie has forgotten her packed lunch so at lunchtime we go to the canteen, where they are serving slime stew with a cardboard lid, otherwise known as pastry.

'Eurgh! No thanks!' shudders Evie, who has slicked down her fringe with lots of water in the cloakroom and looks a little bedraggled. 'And I don't want the curried compost heap, either.'

'At least the school's making an effort with recycling,' I comment. 'The dollop of cold sick on that plate must be stuff they scraped off the plates yesterday and recycled for today's menu.'

'Thanks, Lola. I think I've just lost my appetite – for ever.'

'Look on the bright side – I can't see any Reginald Rooster stuff. Just a large selection of regurgitated yuck.'

As we move along the queue we come to the healthy option, which is a rubbery-looking slice of quiche with a lettuce leaf and some grated carrot. This is also the vegetarian option. Meltonio's eco-friendly ice-cream is on offer too, stored in a nearby fridge-freezer, but the weather feels too cold for ice-cream.

Evie purchases two bananas and, feeling in need of some fresh air, we take our bananas out to the school courtyard and sit shivering on the circular bench under our favourite – now leafless – tree. People are standing huddled together in little groups, stamping their feet to keep warm.

'Hey, I've had a really good idea!' Evie exclaims suddenly, between mouthfuls of banana.

'It's too cold for ideas,' I mumble.

'No, it's a seriously good idea!' Evie continues,

enthusiastically. 'Why don't we set up our own food stall at breaktimes, selling fresh, healthy, locally-sourced, organic, vegetarian snacks? I'm sure it would be really popular, and if our sales are good enough and we make a huge profit, we could buy our own island in the sun and make an eco-resort. And everything on our stall will be totally free-range! We could call it Freshstuff!'

'Freshstuff! I like that! But how could it all be free-range? You don't get free-range bananas!'

'The bananas would be Fair Trade. Not like these.' She brandishes her banana skin. 'I don't think the bananas in the school canteen are Fair Trade.'

'And locally produced? Who do we know who grows bananas?'

'No one. But at least they'd be Fair Trade ones from sustainable crops supporting Third World farmers. Why are you obsessing about bananas?' she adds, in huffy tones. 'I'm trying to get you interested in a really great idea, and all you can talk about is bananas.'

There is an awkward pause, and then we both speak together in a rush.

'It's not that I don't think it's a great idea, Evie. But it might be more difficult than you think. I'm not sure whether we'll ever be able to afford to buy an island. I'm just worried because I know how excited you get about things, and then when they don't work out, you get really disappointed.'

' . . . and it's going to be so cool – it's the best idea I've had for ages!' Evie concludes. I'm not sure what else she said because we were both speaking at the same time, and she obviously wasn't listening to what I was saying.

She has already jumped up and approached a group of our friends to test out her idea on them.

'So what do you think?' she asks eagerly. 'A healthy snack stall, right here in the school. We could call it Freshstuff!'

'Would it be expensive?' Cassia asks, doubtfully.

'No – not if we can help it. We want to keep our costs down by sourcing the cheapest local ingredients we can find. And local produce is fresher and you get more seasonal variety – and it would all be homemade.'

'Yummy homemade cakes!' exclaims Ellen, a little more enthusiastically. 'I love homemade cake stalls!'

'It wouldn't just be cake,' says Evie. 'There'd be other stuff, too. Healthy stuff.'

'Like what?' asks Salma.

'Er . . . like . . . um . . . beanburgers,' says Evie, unconvincingly.

I am not sure what beanburgers are, or how we would make or supply them. The others are looking equally doubtful.

'I don't like baked beans,' says Salma.

'There'd be other stuff, too!' I add, brightly, as I don't

like to see Evie struggling. 'Really nice stuff – and organic, which means it wouldn't contain any chemicals or pesticides, so it would be better for you and taste better too! We're in the early planning stages.'

In the end, everyone agrees that Freshstuff sounds like a good idea. Shaheen and Aisha, who have joined us, are especially enthusiastic as they are both vegetarian. They tell us about some delicious vegetarian recipes which they know, and my mouth begins to water. Shaheen's mother's vegetarian curry with coconut might be difficult to sell at our stall, but Shaheen offers to bring in some lentil samosas and some Indian sweets for people to try.

We even manage to corner Mrs Balderdash, the head teacher, before the end of the day, in order to ask her permission. I am now being swept along on the irresistible wave that is Evie's enthusiasm, and Shaheen and Aisha have inspired me to think that being a vegetarian might not be too bad after all, if I can get Mum to try some new recipes. I'm sure she has a vegetarian cookery book somewhere.

Mrs Balderdash tells us that we can set up a stall as long as we clearly list all the ingredients on everything we sell, and we are not allowed to sell anything that should be kept chilled.

'It looks like beanburgers are off the menu,' I whisper to Evie.

Mrs Balderdash looks at us over the top of the pince-nez glasses perched on her beaky nose. Her eyes twinkle in a kindly fashion. 'I see no harm in a nice little cake stall during breaktime,' she says. 'I might even visit you myself.' She bustles away, her stiff tweed suit rustling slightly around her ample frame.

'Cake! Now everyone's obsessed with cake!' Evie exclaims. 'What is it with people at this school? Has no one heard of fruit or vegetables or healthy grains?' But she doesn't seem at all discouraged.

'What's the hurry?' I gasp, as I run to keep up with Evie when we leave school later on, struggling through the cold gusts of wind under a steel-grey sky. This is different – Evie often has to run to keep up with me! I usually jog to school and back as part of my pre-Olympic training, but this afternoon I am feeling tired and was hoping to walk.

'It's the war on waste!' Evie calls back to me over her shoulder. 'And we can start by not wasting time! Oh bother! I forgot to ask Mr Woodsage if I could borrow that chicken film to show Liam. Never mind, I'll ask tomorrow.'

'But where are we going?' I ask, as Evie has turned the opposite way to our normal route home.

'We're going to source ingredients!'

'Where?'

'Down at the allotments. Maybe we'll find Meltonio there, and he might help us out with some fresh fruit and vegetables! They're packed with vitamins, minerals and antioxidants – all the good stuff you need to keep your body healthy!'

'You're right!' I call back. As an aspiring Olympic athlete, I need to eat a healthy diet. But I am not sure how many fruit and vegetables will be growing at this time of year. 'Er, but – Evie? Isn't it the wrong time of year?' I query, but my words are lost in a sudden gust of cold November drizzle, which sweeps into our faces and whistles past our ears. I am certain that Meltonio will not be at the allotments.

To my surprise I am wrong. He *is* there, digging over a square patch of brown earth, fully clad in bright yellow waterproofs and green wellies. His ice-cream van is parked at the side of the road a short distance away.

'Hi, Meltonio!'

'Oh!' Meltonio jumps, and looks up, startled, from beneath the brim of his bright yellow hat. Then his face creases into a big, happy beam. 'What a surprise!' he exclaims. 'How nice of you to visit on such a miserable day! You have brought sunshine into my day with your presence! Is there a reason why you are here?'

We explain about the healthy food stall, and Evie asks Meltonio if he can spare any fruit or vegetables. I feel slightly embarrassed, asking Meltonio for ingredients, but he doesn't seem to mind. He is even apologetic for the fact that it is the wrong time of year – which is not his fault – and he doesn't have very much, apart from sprouts, leeks, onions, ruby chard and celeriac.

Evie and I exchange doubtful looks. I am not sure how we are going to make healthy, appetising snacks out of root vegetables and a few sprouts. Sprout Surprise? Lush Leeks? Ooh La La Onions? And as for celeriac: I'm a Celeriac – Get Me Out of Here!

'Hang on a minute,' says Meltonio. 'I might have something in the shed.' He disappears into his potting shed and reappears holding two medium-sized pumpkins.

'I've been piling my pumpkins on the shed floor where they won't get nipped on frosty nights,' Meltonio tells us. 'You can have one of these, if you like. This other one is no good.' He shows us one of the pumpkins. 'It is going squashy in the middle. Rotten. So I will take it home for Samson. He loves squashy pumpkin.'

'Who is Samson?' I ask. I know that Meltonio has lots of children, but I can't imagine that he would feed any of them rotten pumpkin.

'Ah! You have not met my Samson!' Meltonio exclaims, his black moustache rippling over a wide smile. 'He is a fine fellow! A pig of distinction!'

'A pig! You've got a pig?' I ask. 'Oh, I love pigs! They're so cool!'

'I love pigs too!' Evie chimes in. 'Can we meet him – please?'

I feel embarrassed again, this time about inviting ourselves. But Meltonio seems perfectly happy. 'I've finished here for the day,' he says. The rain is getting heavier, and it is now quite dark. 'Soon I will have to go to Luigi's to help my brother with the cooking. But there is just time for you to come to my house to meet Samson now, if you would like to.'

'Oh, yes! Please! That would be so cool!' we chorus.

'You had better ask your mothers first,' Meltonio suggests. 'I can drop you back home afterwards, if they say yes. Do you want to use my mobile?'

'It's OK – I've got one,' says Evie, fishing her phone from the bottom of her bag. I have left mine at home. There is just enough credit left for us each to phone home. Our mums sound surprised, but they are happy for us to go, as they know Meltonio well. They ask us to be home in time for tea.

It feels strange, gliding along in the battery-powered ice-cream van in the dark and pouring rain. Meltonio has switched off the ice-cream van's jingle for the winter, which is just as well as it tends to play at the wrong speed as the van's battery runs down. But it is very quiet in the van without it – there is just the swishing of the rain, the soft *whump whump* of the windscreen wiper, and the sound of Meltonio singing to himself.

Evie asks what kind of pig Samson is. 'He's a Gloucester Old Spot,' Meltonio replies. 'It's a breed which is well suited to living out of doors, and very friendly – he has a great personality. Ah! We are nearly there!'

We have not been to Meltonio's house before.

'I live at number twelve Hill Rise – Casa Meltonio,' he says, as the van struggles uphill towards our destination.

Meltonio's house is a three-storey redbrick house, along a row of other redbrick houses.

'My brother Luigi – he lives at number eleven,' says Meltonio, as he ushers us into his home to introduce us to his family. We meet Mrs Meltonio and a crowd of mini Meltonios, who rush up to greet their father with hugs and excited cries of 'Papa! Papa!' He scoops up the smallest one, a tiny girl called Domenica, who nestles against him. He hands her to his wife before taking us into the back garden to meet Samson. We are accompanied by two of the boys.

'They all love Samson,' says Meltonio.

The garden is long and narrow, with apple trees at the far end. 'You see my orchard?' says Meltonio, shining a large torch towards it. 'It is just right for Samson. Pigs love orchards. They fertilise the earth and eat up the windfalls.' Meltonio stops and shines his torch around to show us the large enclosure he has made for Samson. There is pig netting fixed to strong posts to stop Samson escaping into the rest of the garden.

'My wife would not be happy if Samson ate her flowers and turned the lawn into a quagmire!' Meltonio says with a laugh. 'Now – where is he? Probably in his house, keeping warm and dry. Sensible pig. Ah! Here he is! He has seen the torch, and is coming to say hello and find out if we have brought him something nice and tasty. He loves his food!'

'Oh, wow!' I exclaim, and Evie hugs me in excitement as a large pink pig with black spots on his broad back first pokes his pink snout out of his pig arc – a basic hut made from curved corrugated iron – and then emerges fully and trots towards us, grunting gently. He nuzzles Meltonio's outstretched flat palm with his moist snout, and the two boys lean over the netting to stroke him. Evie and I join in. Meltonio shines his torch to provide light so that Evie can take photos of Samson on her phone.

'He's lovely and warm,' she whispers, keeping her voice low so that she doesn't alarm the pig.

'I love his shiny coat,' I say. 'He's so cool!'

Meltonio drops the rotten pumpkin right into the enclosure and Samson starts snuffling at it and gobbling noisily.

'How often do you feed him?' I ask.

'Twice a day. He gets pig nuts, soaked barley meal with milk, soya and fruit and vegetable scraps, like this pumpkin. But he must have his potatoes cooked, or he gets ill. And he digs and forages for worms and nutrients in the soil and grass. He gets his water from that large tin bucket over there – I had to fix it to the ground because he kept knocking it over. And look – that muddy hollow over there is the pig puddle. That's where he likes to wallow and take a bath. I top it up with the hose every day. But I also put a wooden floor in his little house so he can sleep in deep straw away from damp earth. He is a very pampered pig!'

'Where did he come from?' Evie asks. 'I never knew you had a pig!'

'Ah! Until recently he lived on a farm where my friend who breeds pigs raised him from a piglet. So he lived with his mother and his brothers and his sisters, and now he has come to live with me, until Christmas.'

'Oh – where is he going at Christmas?' I ask.

Meltonio looks at me, his thick dark eyebrows raised, as if surprised by my question. 'At Christmas we will eat him,' he replies, quietly.

'Oh! You . . . are . . . going . . . to . . . to . . . to . . .' My voice trails away, and I feel as though an invisible icy hand is clutching at my throat. I can't bear the thought of such a beautiful pig getting eaten! How can Meltonio possibly even think of . . . of . . .

'Eat him – that's right.' Meltonio calls softly to Samson, reaching out his hand to stroke him.

'No!' exclaims Evie in horror. 'You can't do that! He's your friend!'

'I know! I know!' says Meltonio, chuckling. 'I must not get too attached to him – but I can't help it. At least I am giving him a happy life. Healthy, happy pigs grow into tasty pigs.' He sighs. 'But it will still be hard to part with him.'

Samson has finished his pumpkin and suddenly rears up, placing his front trotters on a fence post while Meltonio fondles his ears. 'Look how bright his eyes are,' Meltonio says, lifting up Samson's floppy ears to show us his little eyes. 'Bright eyes are a sign of health. So is a nice curly tail. A straight tail means that a pig is sick. Oh dear, I don't mean to upset you. Your mothers will not be pleased with me.' Meltonio looks concerned, but I think he is more worried about upsetting Evie and me than he is about eating Samson.

'Do you *have* to eat him?' I ask in a small voice. I feel so sad. Samson is so beautiful, and so . . . alive. It doesn't seem right to end his life – it ISN'T right!

Meltonio sighs. 'These Gloucester Old Spots are traditionally kept in this way, in orchards or gardens, and fattened up on scraps for Christmas. They lay down a lot of fat – the crackling from these pigs is unbelievable, it is so good . . .'

But Evie has covered her ears.

'Perhaps I had better take you home now,' says Meltonio, looking awkward. 'Try to remember that Samson is a happy pig – he is having the best life a pig can have . . .'

We are very quiet on the journey home. Cradling the pumpkin on my lap, I notice tears glistening on Evie's cheeks. I feel like crying, too. Meltonio is becoming increasingly worried, trying to convince us that it is better to eat a happy pig than to buy intensively-farmed unhappy turkeys and chickens for Christmas. I suppose he has a point.

I manage to pull myself together sufficiently in order to thank Meltonio and ask if we can visit him and see Samson again – before Christmas.

'Of course! Of course!' Meltonio cries, obviously relieved that I am not falling apart.

But Evie gets out of the van and goes into her house without another word.

Eco-info

By the time all the ingredients that make
a Christmas dinner arrive on your plate,
they will typically have travelled a combined
distance of 49000 miles.

To help reduce the carbon cost of food at
Christmas - and all year round too - try to buy
as much locally-produced food as possible and a
free-range or, better still, organic turkey -
10 million are eaten every Christmas so make sure
they've been reared in good conditions.

Chapter Three

I have to go home for my tea, but I text Evie to ask if I can come round to see her afterwards, as I am worried about her. She texts back to say yes.

After depositing the pumpkin in my room, I find Mum and Dad sitting at the table waiting for me. 'It's your favourite, dear,' says Mum. 'Sausages!'

I think about Samson – I look at the sausages – I think about Samson being turned into sausages – I burst into tears.

'Oh dear, whatever is the matter?' says Mum, hurrying over to put her arm round me.

I tell Mum and Dad about Samson, and how Meltonio is going to kill and eat him for Christmas.

'Mmm! Crackling!' says Dad, licking his lips.

This doesn't help.

Mum tells him off for not being more sensitive. He

apologises, and says that he knows it's hard but I should try not to get too attached to Samson.

'But I want to save him!' I howl miserably.

Dad says that he can understand my wish to 'save the bacon', as he puts it – but it may not be possible.

'Come and have your tea, dear,' Mum coaxes me. I make an effort to pull myself together and not to cry. I tell Mum that I am now a vegetarian.

Mum looks doubtful, and says that she hopes that I am going to eat properly and get enough protein in my diet.

'Don't worry, Mum,' I reply. 'I'll make sure I eat properly. A healthy balanced diet is really important when you're training for the Olympics. Could you look for that vegetarian cookery book and maybe try out some of the recipes? I'm sure they will have all the right nutrients, as well as being delicious – hopefully.' I pause for breath as I am gabbling slightly, trying not to think about sausages, or look at them . . . 'Cheese is a good source of protein,' I continue. 'Can I make some cheese on toast?'

Mum says I can. I overhear Dad whispering to her that I am unlikely, in his opinion, to stay vegetarian for long. I decide to remain a vegetarian until the day I die, just to prove him wrong. I just wish the sausages didn't smell so good.

I am annoyed with Dad for not being more

supportive, and eat my cheese on toast in moody silence, darting him the occasional glowering look. He is growing a scraggly beard and looks like a Father Christmas who's down on his luck.

'Is there anything wrong, Lola?' he asks me eventually.

Apart from everything? 'No,' I say. Then I ask him if he has any fruit and vegetables in the garden. He tells me that it is the wrong time of year, and all he has are a few sprouts. The last of the carrots were eaten by carrot root fly and slugs because I wouldn't let him use any pesticides, which are bad for the environment and get into the food which people eat.

'Organic food is much better,' I remind Dad. 'It's chemical-free so it doesn't harm or even kill living things. I'd hate to think of any birds or other little creatures getting poisoned. Organic food production promotes biodiversity,' I add, remembering a lesson with Mr Woodsage.

'I don't know about biodiversity,' says Dad. 'It's certainly very good for slugs – I've never seen so many!'

It sounds like he is trying to blame me for this, which is so unfair! I give him a hard stare.

'So where do you get fresh organic vegetarian stuff at this time of year?' I ask.

'The supermarket?' Mum suggests. 'But it's expensive, as I keep telling you.'

'You could try the Saturday farmers' market,' says Dad. 'That's quite good – and not too overpriced.'

This is actually a good idea, although I don't want to admit it as I am still not pleased with Dad for doubting my ability to remain vegetarian – even though he is probably right . . .

I ask if I can go round to see Evie. Mum tells me not to be too long as I am looking tired.

Dad's new bicycle is parked in the hall. He has recently started cycling in order to keep fit and, he tells me proudly, to reduce his carbon footprint. I am pleased that he is getting the message to go green, although I don't like to be around when he puts on his bicycle helmet and cycling shorts as he looks like a stick insect with its head stuck in a goldfish bowl.

'What's wrong?' Evie and I both say to each other instantly as she opens the door to let me in. We hug each other.

'Dad's been giving me a hard time,' I say. 'And I keep thinking about Samson.'

'Liam's winding me up,' says Evie. 'And I can't stop thinking about Samson too. I thought I wouldn't be able to face eating anything because I'm so upset about poor Samson, but then I decided that it's important to keep my strength up so that I can think of a way to save him – I need brain food! And I don't want to let

Liam put me off with his stupid remarks which don't help!'

'I thought Liam would be at work.'

'It's his evening off – unfortunately.'

Evie's mum calls her from the kitchen to come and finish her cheese on toast.

'That's what I had!' I say.

'Oh, really? How funny!' says Evie. 'Cheese on toast is OK, but I can't wait for Mum to get round to making her vegetable lasagne, and I also want her to make cheese, lentil and tomato bake, which is seriously delicious.'

Liam is in the kitchen, frying bacon.

'He's doing it deliberately just to upset me,' says Evie. 'I should never have told him about Samson.'

'I just fancied a bacon sandwich – OK?' Liam snaps at her. 'Is there a law against it?'

'I'm sure Liam doesn't want to upset you, dear,' says her mum.

'He certainly wouldn't do it deliberately,' says her dad.

'OK – my parents are seriously deluded,' Evie remarks. 'Their darling son can do no wrong.'

'That's enough, Evie.'

I sit down on a kitchen chair a little gingerly, not wishing to be caught up in the middle of a family argument. I send thought waves to Evie to hurry up and finish her cheese on toast, so that we can escape to her room. I don't like it when she argues with Liam – I like Liam, and can usually see his side of the argument. Being an only child I am not used to arguing with anyone – apart from Dad – and I really hate it on the rare occasions when Evie and I fall out. I am also suffering severely mixed feelings because the bacon which Liam is frying is reminding me of Samson, but it also smells *wonderful*! Oh no! My mouth is watering! I must *not* start drooling . . .

In order to take my mind off the bacon I tell Evie about Dad's idea to go to the farmers' market – although I make it sound as though it was *my* idea.

'We can get loads of fresh ingredients for our stall,' I say hopefully, even though I have never actually been to a farmers' market before. 'And it's not too overpriced. And we'll be supporting local farmers.'

'That's a really good idea,' Evie agrees. 'When's it on?'

'Saturday morning – in the marketplace,' says Evie's mum. 'I might ask you to get some carrots – the ones in our garden got eaten by carrot root fly because Evie said we shouldn't use any insecticides. And the slugs ate a lot of the other vegetables.'

'Dad's carrots got eaten too,' I say.

Liam sits down at the table with his bacon sandwich. I try not to look, in case I drool – partly over the bacon sandwich, partly over Liam . . .

'So everyone's carrots got gobbled up by little flies and the slugs had a great time chomping everything because of your obsession with going organic,' says Liam, between mouthfuls. 'You're not just organic – you're manic!'

'But surely it's better to eat organic stuff which is free from chemicals?' Evie argues.

Liam shrugs. 'The slugs don't seem to mind, so why should I?' he says. 'I don't care if carrots are organic, non-organic or made from pure love and moonbeams and harvested when Venus is aligned with Mars. A carrot is a carrot.'

'And a pig is a pig,' Evie retorts. 'Samson's a pig – and so are you. But Samson's a much nicer pig.'

'Perhaps I'll come and meet him one day,' says Liam.

'You should,' says Evie. 'You'd have a lot in common. Samson's always guzzling in a trough.'

'Wow! This is a seriously good bacon sandwich!' Liam enthuses, eyeing his sister. 'Want some, sis?'

Evie makes a noise of disgust and scrapes back her chair. 'I've heard that Britain is the dustbin of Europe because of the amount of rubbish we send to landfill,' she says. 'If that's true, then Liam is definitely the dustbin of the UK! Come on, Lola – let's go! Let's leave the Carbon Monster emitting CO_2 from every orifice!'

I take it that she means Liam.

'Excuse me!' Liam calls after her. 'Vegetables make you fart even more!'

'Liam!' exclaims their mum reprovingly.

'But it's true!' I hear Liam saying as we run up the stairs. 'And as well as generating tonnes of extra gas, if this country grew enough locally-sourced fruit and veg to provide everyone with the five portions we're meant to scoff a day, the whole of the UK would be covered in polytunnels . . .'

Again, I can see his side of the argument.

Evie shuts her bedroom door firmly so that we can no longer hear Liam railing against the scourge of the green meanies – like us.

Evie flumps down on her bed. 'So what are we going to do about Samson?' she asks. 'We have *got* to save him.'

'Agreed. I just don't know how.'

Evie narrows her eyes and looks thoughtful. 'I know! We could form the Pig Liberation Front! We could go there in the middle of the night with wire-cutters, wearing black balaclavas, and —'

'Get arrested?'

'Probably,' Evie concedes.

'And even if we didn't get arrested, what would we do with Samson once we'd liberated him? What do you do with a liberated pig?' I ask.

Evie shrugs. 'So much for Plan A,' she says.

'What's Plan B?' I ask.

Evie shrugs again and pulls a face. 'I don't know,' she says. 'You tell me.'

I scratch my head. 'Perhaps we could persuade Meltonio to become a vegetarian.'

Evie looks sceptical. 'Do you really think Meltonio would become a vegetarian?'

'He might.'

'And pigs might fly,' says Evie, dryly.

'We've got to try.'

'We haven't got very long to persuade him. Christmas is coming and Samson's getting fat.'

'So we need to get to work! Come on, Evie! Let's plan some vegetarian food to sell at our stall at school and to tempt Meltonio to switch to vegetarianism!'

Evie throws herself face down on to her bed and screams into her pillow. Then she looks up at me, slightly flushed in the face, her red curls tumbling haphazardly around her shoulders.

'I don't know!' she exclaims. 'I don't know if we can do any of it! I don't know if we can save Samson, and I can't bear the thought of . . . of . . .'

'Don't think about it,' I say firmly. 'We *will* save Samson – somehow. And the healthy food stall was your idea – remember? Are you having second thoughts?'

Evie sits up and smoothes down her hair. 'I'm sorry,' she says. 'I think I'm just tired. And Liam's got me all wound up. And I don't really want to fall out with him because he's OK, really, for a brother. He helped us loads with the Tree-aid concert. And I want to go on having guitar lessons!'

'Take some deep breaths.'

Evie inhales and exhales loudly. 'Thanks, Lola.' She looks at me. 'You're so good at calming me down.'

'I can help you with plenty of stress-busting techniques,' I say. 'Exercise is good. You should come with me on some of my pre-Olympic training runs and swims.'

'Maybe I will. I might start cycling as well.'

'Good idea. I'll get my bike out, too. I just hope Dad doesn't want to come with us . . .'

'Oh, why not?' says Evie. 'Your poor dad – you're so mean! Anyway, the family which cycles and recycles together, stays together – didn't you know?' She has gone over to the computer.

'What are you doing?'

'Looking up healthy vegetarian recipes . . . Here's one: goat's cheese and sun-dried tomato tartlet – yum!'

'I don't like goat's cheese. And we couldn't use that one, anyway. We're not allowed to sell anything that should be kept chilled – remember?'

'So what can we sell?'

'There must be loads of things. We can offer simple things like freshly-dug organic carrots. Carrots are so good for you.'

'I hardly think that people are going to flock to our stall if it's laden with nothing but carrots, especially if they're covered with earth! And do you really think that if we offer Meltonio a raw carrot he'll instantly throw up his hands, shout "Hallelujah!" and switch to vegetarianism?'

'OK! OK! So *you* suggest something!' I exclaim, folding my arms defensively.

'Don't be offended, Lola!' says Evie. 'We could make carrot cake,' she adds, appeasingly.

'OK,' I say. 'But not everyone likes it – although I do.'

'You like *every* kind of cake,' Evie points out, laughing.

'True. But what does *everyone* like?'

'Chocolate,' says Evie firmly. 'People like chocolate. And dark chocolate is good for you. We could use organic Fairtrade chocolate. Why don't we make dark chocolate cornflake cakes?'

'Yum! They sound good! I'm sure they'd be very popular. We could use branflakes instead of cornflakes to make them healthier.'

'Good idea!' Evie agrees. 'Dark chocolate branflake cakes. Mum's got loads of branflakes in the cupboard.'

She is still gazing at the computer screen. 'There are loads of vegetarian recipes,' she remarks. 'Cheese and onion bread pudding – that sounds OK. And flatbread, feta and chickpea salad sounds interesting. How about roast peppers stuffed with cheese, rice and pine nuts? Mmm! That sounds good! Or filled baked potatoes – I love those!'

'Evie,' I moan. 'Stop! I've just eaten but you're making me hungry again. Oh! I've had a brilliant idea!'

'What – even better than chocolate branflake cakes?'

'It's not a recipe. I just thought of a way of getting Meltonio to turn vegetarian. We could show him the chicken film. He loves animals —'

'He loves *eating* animals!'

'Yes – but he also likes to see them being looked after properly. The chicken film would really shock him. And then we could try to persuade him to become a vegetarian, like us. It's got to be worth a try!'

'I suppose so. I'm just worried that nothing's going to turn Meltonio vegetarian. He doesn't look remotely like a vegetarian. Vegetarians are usually skinny.'

'Not always. Anyway, are you going to ask Mr Woodsage if we can borrow the film tomorrow?'

'Definitely. I certainly want to show it to Liam!'

There is a pause and Evie twists one of her curls around her finger.

'Have you got any chocolate?' I ask. 'Talking about chocolate just now has made me want some.'

'There may be some in the kitchen. There's all sorts of stuff in the cupboards. Let's go down and search – we can source ingredients.'

We go down to the kitchen and Evie gets down on her hands and knees and delves into one of the cupboards. She finds some dark chocolate and some dark cocoa. She also finds, among other things, a multi-pack of Mr Porky pork scratchings.

'Oh – yuck!' she exclaims. 'These must be Liam's. They're revolting!' She peers at the list of ingredients. 'They're made from pork rind and monosodium glutamate and loads of additives. How horrible is that?' She pulls a being-sick face.

'At least Samson won't end up as pork scratchings,' I remark, and then wish I hadn't. Evie looks as if she is going to cry.

'And there's so much packaging!' I exclaim, trying to steer the conversation away from Samson. 'It's so wasteful – all those little bags inside a big bag.'

'You know why there's so much extra packaging these days?' asks Liam, coming into the kitchen to fetch a drink from the fridge.

I shake my head.

'It's because of regulations forcing manufacturers to list all the ingredients and nutritional information on all their products, and so they need extra space and therefore extra packaging in order to do that.'

'But I want to know what's in my food,' I say.

'Exactly,' says Liam. 'So you can't win.' He takes a swig from a carton of fruit smoothie. 'Did you know that the longest recorded flight of a chicken is thirteen seconds?' he asks me.

I shake my head again.

Liam drops the empty fruit smoothie carton into the bin.

'Put that in the recycling bin!' Evie barks at him fiercely.

Liam looks mock offended. 'You really should be nicer to me,' he says. 'I'm the wonderful brother whose band played at your Tree-aid concert recently and helped you raise lots of money for poor starving trees in the Third World.'

'I know,' says Evie in a calmer voice. 'And I'm really grateful for that. But it doesn't mean that you don't have to recycle. People should re-use and recycle more. Reduce, reuse and recycle – the three Rs.'

Liam rolls his eyes. 'Oh, here we go again!' he says. 'See this lid from that empty bottle of fabric conditioner over there?' He picks it up. 'Why not fashion it into a hat to keep out the cold, which will also allow you to save money on your gas bill and reduce your carbon footprint?'

I start giggling. Evie is trying not to look amused, but I notice her lips twitching . . .

> ### Eco-info
> Almost seventy-five per cent of the rubbish generated in an average household is due to packaging. Try not to choose highly-packaged food - such as invidivually wrapped packs - and reuse packaging like drinks bottles as much possible.

Chapter Four

'What should we do with all the money we raise from our healthy food stall?' I ask, as we walk to school the following day, which is Friday. We have decided to visit the farmers' market tomorrow morning, and then spend the rest of the weekend cooking and preparing delicious organic food in order to set up our first Freshstuff stall on Monday.

'I think we should start a Save Samson the Pig Fund,' says Evie. 'We could use it to persuade Meltonio to buy something else to eat for Christmas – or we could buy Samson from him.'

'Where would we keep him?'

'I could ask Dad to make a pig enclosure.' Evie sounds doubtful. 'It was difficult enough persuading Mum and Dad to let me have two goldfish. I don't know about a pig. Do you think your parents would have him?'

'I doubt it.' I crane my neck to look at the photos of Samson which Evie is looking at on her phone. I need to wear glasses for reading, but I can see the photos without them. They are a bit dark but I can see his pink snout and floppy ears – he is so cute!

'Oh well – we can think about that later on,' says Evie. 'I really want to take Liam to meet Samson over the weekend. I know he'd like him.'

'Can I come?'

'Of course! Brrr! Isn't it cold?' Evie claps her gloved hands together.

'Yes – it's freezing! I like your gloves, by the way – purple is such a cool colour.'

'Thanks – they're made from pure yak's wool. Mum sells them in Fashion Passion. She's got loads of great new stuff in her shop at the moment – let's go there together soon! I like your leg-warmers. The light grey looks really good over your black tights.'

'I'm doing everything I can to keep warm at the moment,' I say. 'I asked Mum and Dad not to turn the heating right up because I didn't want our carbon footprint to get huge – so I'm having to think of other ways to keep warm.'

'Like wearing lots of layers of clothes?'

'Yes – and I've put silver foil behind the radiators to reflect heat back into the rooms, and I keep my curtains drawn to shut out draughts and stop heat escaping through the windows. And then, when I'd done all that, I found Mum sneakily turning up the thermostat!'

Evie sighs heavily. 'Parents can be a major obstacle in the fight against global warming, can't they?'

'They certainly can! I keep asking Dad to draught-proof the letterbox – but he *still* hasn't got round to it!'

'I know what you mean. I keep telling Dad that it will only take him two and a half hours to insulate the loft with sheep's fleece, and a further half hour to fit a new insulating jacket around the hot water tank – but can he be bothered?'

'Keep telling him that it will save him money – the thought of reducing their energy bills is what gets them most excited. Don't give up! Eco-worriers united will defeat the eco-monsters in the end!'

'What are you doing, Lola?' Evie asks.

'I'm picking up fir cones.'

'I can see that. Why?'

'To make Christmas decorations. Making your own decorations is more eco-friendly than buying them. I really want to find some holly.'

'It's December the first tomorrow.'

'I know! Isn't it exciting? It's nearly Christmas! Do you think it will snow?'

Evie shakes her head sadly. 'It doesn't feel very Christmassy to me. And I don't want to think about

Christmas because of Samson . . .'

'Oh . . . sorry . . . I forgot . . .' I feel awkward and ashamed of forgetting about poor Samson. 'It probably won't snow because of global warming,' I say, trying to change the subject. 'We only get rain these days.'

Evie still looks sad.

'We'll celebrate when we've saved Samson, shall we?' I say, trying to sound a positive note.

Evie nods, and smiles wanly.

'What have you brought for lunch today?' I ask Evie. It is lunchbreak and we are sitting underneath our favourite tree.

'I've got cheese sandwiches made with Dad's sun-dried tomato and herb bread, an apple and a bag of pomegranate seeds. I chopped up a pomegranate this morning. The seeds are just like little sweets – only healthier. Try some!' She offers me the bag. I take a few little ruby red seeds. 'Pomegranates are a superfood. We should have them on our stall.'

'Good idea!' The pomegranate seeds are delicious.

Evie asks me what I've brought for lunch.

'Cheese sandwiches,' I reply. 'Two grapes. And an apple. I think it's organic, but Mum peels the little labels off. She tells me the apples are organic, but she may be cheating and getting ordinary ones to save money.'

'That's terrible!'

'Do you think your dad would make some of his special bread for our stall?'

'He might.'

We sit in silence, munching our cheese sandwiches. My eyes are irresistibly drawn to two boys who are standing nearby and tucking into jumbo sausage rolls.

'Stop eyeing up the boys, Lola!' says Evie, nudging me and giggling.

I don't like to say that I am eyeing up their sausage rolls rather than the boys themselves. I am finding vegetarianism a challenge – last night I dreamed that I was tucking into a huge plate of roast chicken with all the trimmings, and when I woke up there was a little trickle of drool dribbling from the corner of my mouth. Even though I like vegetarian food, I can't help missing meat.

Evie seems to read my mind. 'Are you getting carnal cravings?' she asks. 'Before I became a vegetarian I didn't crave meat. Now that I'm not allowed it, I keep wanting it!'

'Me too!'

'Apart from sausages,' says Evie. 'I don't care if I never eat another sausage, or bacon, or anything related to a pig. I've been put right off because of Samson.'

'Oh – me too!' I say again, trying to keep my eyes

averted from the jumbo sausage rolls.

Evie pats my arm gently. 'Never mind – we can encourage each other when our vegetarian spirits flag or our carnal appetites threaten to get the better of us.'

'Did you get the chicken film from Mr Woodsage?' I ask.

'Yes. He said I could borrow it for the weekend. It's in my bag.'

Cassia, Ellen and Salma are walking over.

'Let's tell them about Samson!' says Evie, jumping up and going to greet them.

'Do you want to see Samson?' Evie asks, getting out her phone.

'Who's Samson?' Ellen asks.

'This is Samson!'

'Oh, wow! He is seriously cute! Whose pig is he? Where did you meet him?'

Evie and I tell them all about Samson, and they are horrified to hear about Meltonio's plan to turn Samson into Christmas dinner. Cassia gives a shriek when she hears about this, and they all exclaim and shout 'NO!' so loudly that other people start drifting over to find out what is going on.

Soon we have attracted quite a crowd, and everyone wants to meet Samson and persuade Meltonio not to eat him.

Amelia sashays across the courtyard, followed by

Jemima and the So Cool Girls and peers over Evie's shoulder at the photos of Samson.

'Eurgh! Gross! It's a pig! They smell!'

'They only smell if their owners don't look after them,' I retort. 'Pigs are very clean creatures, and very intelligent. They're a lot more intelligent than you!'

This is quite rude, but Amelia has made me cross.

She pinches her lips together and her nostrils go all narrow.

'Trust you to make friends with a pig!' she spits at us like an angry cat. 'You're two sad losers whose only friend is a pig!'

'Get lost, Amelia!' chorus Cassia, Ellen, Salma, Skye, Megan, Tegan, Karlie, Chelsey, Yasmin, Aisha, Gemma, Victoria, Dannii and Shaheen – and Lee, Harry, Eddie and Jack, who have also joined the crowd of Samson admirers.

Amelia slinks away, sneering at us over her shoulder. The So Cool Girls follow her like shadows, sneering in unison.

'Can we come with you to meet Samson?' Cassia asks.

'Ooh, yes,' says Ellen, enthusiastically. 'That would be über-cool!'

'I don't think we can all go,' I say nervously, looking at the large, eager crowd. 'We can't just turn up . . .'

Fortunately, several people say that they can't go

anyway – and then some others decide that they wouldn't be able to, either.

'Don't forget to buy fresh stuff from our stall on Monday,' Evie calls after them. 'It'll boost your brain power and boost your body's natural defences – and you'll be supporting the Save Samson Fund!'

But Cassia, Ellen, Megan, Lee and Jack are still keen to meet Samson.

'I don't know if we can just invite ourselves,' I mutter to Evie. 'It seems rude to turn up uninvited.'

'But Meltonio won't mind,' Evie argues. 'He's really friendly. And bringing people with us might help to convince him not to eat Samson. You do *want* to save Samson, don't you?' She narrows her eyes and gives me a hard stare.

'Of *course* I do!' I exclaim, feeling offended that she could possible think I didn't. 'OK – we'll go! After school today – meet us at the school gates and we'll take you to meet a very special pig!'

Cassia, Ellen, Megan, Lee and Jack cheer loudly.

It is a long cold walk, but eventually we reach Meltonio's house.

For some reason Amelia and Jemima have decided to trail after us, making rude remarks about pigs and 'losers'.

The others hang back while Evie rings the doorbell.

Fortunately Meltonio is at home and seems surprised, but pleased, to see us all.

'Of course! Of course! Your friends must meet Samson! He loves having visitors – he is such a sociable pig. Come along, everyone! You as well!' He beckons to Amelia and Jemima, who exchange doubtful looks and then follow us, hanging back slightly, down the garden. They look as if they have a bad smell under their noses – but they always look like this.

Samson is lying on his side near the pig puddle, half asleep, when we arrive, but he gets up and comes to greet us, grunting and pushing his strong snout against the netting. The girls squeal and exclaim, 'He's so cute!' and everyone pats him, apart from Amelia and Jemima, who hang back. Mrs Meltonio brings a pail of warm slops down the garden, and Meltonio goes into the enclosure to pour them into the trough. Samson trots after him and begins to guzzle happily.

'That is one seriously cool pig,' says Jack admiringly, and everyone agrees.

Behind us we hear a gagging sound. We all turn to see Amelia clutching her stomach and retching.

'Uuurgh!' she says. 'Pigs!' Then she picks up her school bag and runs back up the garden, round the side of the house and out of sight, with Jemima hot on her heels.

'The poor girl is not well,' Meltonio says. 'Should someone go after her?'

'She'll be OK,' says Evie firmly. 'I think she's allergic to pigs.'

Everyone laughs, apart from Meltonio, who still looks worried.

'So why did she come?' he asks.

'Oh, she wanted to make fun of us,' Evie replies. 'But her plans usually backfire. We're used to it – it's OK.'

Samson has trotted back over to the fence, and Meltonio gently scratches his broad back. A few people take photos of the pig on their phones, leaning in as close as possible as the greyish November light is fading fast.

Evie chooses this moment to launch straight into our bid to alter Meltonio's eating habits. 'Have you ever considered becoming a vegetarian?' she asks, giving Meltonio a half-determined, half-appealing look.

Meltonio's moustache quivers with amusement. 'No,' he replies. 'I don't think I would make a good vegetarian!'

'But being a vegetarian is very good for you,' Evie persists. 'It's good for your health as well as being an ethical way of life.'

'It's really good for your figure!' I venture.

Meltonio's eyes twinkle. 'Are you saying I'm fat?' he asks.

'Oh! Er . . . no. No!' I stammer, feeling very embarrassed.

But Meltonio throws back his head and roars with laughter.

I don't think we're doing well at persuading him.

Evie obviously feels that the time has come to use the main weapon in our armoury.

'I've brought a really shocking film about chickens home from school,' says Evie. 'If you watch it, you may begin to think it's not such a bad idea to become a vegetarian. I've got it in my bag.' Evie rummages in her school bag.

Meltonio tells us that unfortunately he has to go to work now so he is unable to watch the film.

'But Luigi's will be closed this Sunday,' he says. 'You and Lola are welcome to come back then – and you can bring your film, if you like. I am a bit busy until then, I am afraid.'

'We'd love to come back on Sunday,' I say, gratefully. 'Can we help you with Samson when we come back?'

'Of course!'

'And would it be all right if I bring my brother to meet Samson?' Evie asks.

'Certainly! That would be splendid! Samson loves to make new friends. He has so enjoyed meeting you all this afternoon!'

We say our goodbyes to Meltonio and to Samson, who grunts in reply.

As we leave, Megan turns back and says to Meltonio, 'Please don't eat him!'

Meltonio opens his mouth as if to say something, but then closes it again. He looks awkward. Then he turns and leans over the fence to stroke Samson's silky ears.

Perhaps we are beginning to get through to him – I hope so! Evie glances at me and smiles.

We are in my room. Evie has dropped in briefly on her way home. We are both feeling more hopeful that Meltonio will not eat Samson in the end.

'We need to keep up the pressure. But I don't want us to get our hopes up only to have them dashed,' I say. 'We'd better not count our chickens before they've hatched!'

'I only want to count happy, free-range chickens,' says Evie. 'So we need to show Meltonio how loved Samson is – by everyone.'

'Apart from Amelia.'

Evie laughs. 'That was so funny!' she exclaims. 'She really doesn't like animals very much, does she?'

'She doesn't like us either.'

'Oh, well – I think we can cope with that.' Evie sits on the bed and looks around my room. 'I like the way you told *me* off for leaving my lights on!' she says indignantly. 'Look at all your fairy lights! And you've left them on all day – how wasteful is that? I thought you were an eco-worrier, like me!'

'I *am*! You know I am! I just forgot to switch them off this morning, that's all,' I say defensively. 'I was in a rush, because I wanted to put out some more nuts for the birds before I left for school – it's really important at this time of year. I don't want the birds to starve! And I only put the lights up late last night, ready for December the first. You can't have Christmas without fairy lights!'

'But you've got so many!'

'Yes – but I couldn't just have *one* fairy light, could I? It would look strange.'

'No – but you could maybe have not quite so many. They do look nice, though. Have you got any chocolate?'

'I think we ate it all at your house. I haven't got any left, I'm afraid. We need to get some tomorrow for our chocolate branflake cakes. I'll have to ask Mum for some money. Do you think your mum will give you any?'

'I expect so, especially if we tell them they're contributing to the Save Samson Fund.'

The smell of roast chicken is beginning to float upstairs from the kitchen.

'Oh no!' I groan. 'That smells sooo good, and I am soooooo hungry! It's not fair! I asked Mum to make vegetarian food – but she said it would be worse to waste the chicken and we'd have to eat that first. But I can't – not if I'm going to be a proper vegetarian like you!'

'Be strong!' says Evie firmly, gripping my arm. 'Think of Samson!'

'Samson's a pig – not a chicken.'

'So think of the chickens in that programme.'

'But some of the chickens in that film were happy – I mean the ones in the second part of the programme. I made Mum promise only to buy happy chickens – the ones with the RSPCA Freedom Food Mark.'

'I don't care if they were happy – that's not a good reason for eating them! How would you like it if I ate you, just because you were happy?'

I groan loudly. 'I can't bear the thought of eating yet another cheese toastie while Mum and Dad tuck into a happy roast chicken! I can't do this, Evie. I'm in training for the next Olympics, and I should be eating a balanced and varied diet.'

Evie seizes my shoulders and looks deep into my eyes. 'Lola,' she says earnestly. 'We promised that we would help each other stick to being vegetarian.'

Did we?

'You can do this, Lola! Keep telling yourself: "I can do this!" Go on – try it.'

'I can do this.' I don't feel or sound very convinced, but Evie seems happy.

'Good girl. And remember – you can call me any time this evening for counselling. I am your personal helpline. OK?'

'OK. Thanks.'

'I must go now,' says Evie. 'Dad said he'd cook me a goat's cheese and sundried tomato tartlet, because Mum hasn't had time to make a veggie lasagne yet.'

'Cool,' I say. 'Enjoy!'

As soon as I am sure that she has gone, I race downstairs and almost fall at Mum's feet, imploring her to forget I ever said anything about being a vegetarian. 'You did get the Freedom Food Mark chickens, didn't you, Mum?' I ask, anxiously. Even in my desperate chicken-starved state, I don't think I could face eating a Reginald Rooster bargain chicken. Mum assures me that the chicken isn't a Reginald Rooster one, and that, as far as she knows, the chicken led a reasonably happy life before it ended up in the supermarket. I really want to believe that this is true – the chicken smells soooo good.

Soon I am devouring a huge plate of roast chicken and all the trimmings. It has never tasted so good! But almost immediately I feel hugely guilty as I don't want to let Evie down – and I really do like a lot of vegetarian food, but the roast chicken was too hard to resist.

'So you're not a vegetarian today,' Dad says, stating the obvious.

'No – I'm not. But pleeease don't tell Evie!'

I am back in my room, listening to 'Running on Water'

by Boys Next Door on my iPod and doing some gentle aerobic and stretching exercises. I still feel guilty about my lapse from vegetarianism – but Evie need never know! I can be mostly vegetarian – but this evening my body told me that I needed roast chicken, and I think it's important to listen to your body. And it definitely wasn't a Reginald Rooster chicken!

My phone rings. It is Evie. 'Do you need counselling?' she asks.

'Probably,' I reply, trying not to sound jumpy or guilty. 'But I'm rather tired – I might just go to bed. I'll come round to your house tomorrow morning and we'll go to the farmers' market. And I was wondering if we might drop in at Luigi's for a drink. Is Liam going to be working there tomorrow?' I ask, trying to make my voice sound über-casual. Unfortunately I think I sound über-eager.

'Yes, he's going to be there. But he's told me on pain of slow and excruciating death not to go there and embarrass him.'

'Oh, but we won't embarrass him! We'll just go there and have a drink.'

'OK.'

'Um ... so ... I'll see you in the morning!'

'Yes. And remember that you can call me anytime, night or day, for counselling.'

'Thanks.'

'Sweet vegetarian dreams!'

'Sweet dreams to you, too!' I endeavour to keep the tinge of guilt out of my voice.

To calm myself down, I relax in a warm bath with a generous amount of my favourite Green Green Bath of Foam from Bodyzone, which is one of my favourite shops as all its products are eco-friendly as well as smelling wonderful!

I turn off my fairy lights before falling gratefully into bed. Before I turn off my phone I see that Evie has sent me a text reminding me that I can call her for counselling ... Would she be totally disgusted if she knew that I am already a lapsed vegetarian? Should I confess? Or maybe, if I am mostly vegetarian, it doesn't matter and what Evie doesn't know won't hurt her.

Eco-info

It's actually more green to be vegetarian. A diet containing meat requires three times the resources (such as energy and land space) as a vegetarian diet.

Chapter Five

'He called you what?!'

Evie and I are on our way to the farmers' market. It is a beautiful crisp sunny day, a welcome relief after all the November dreariness, and I am enjoying the walk and looking out for birds such as pied wagtails, which are winter visitors. Mum said that the forecast is for rain later, but I find it hard to believe so I am wearing a short denim skirt over black tights and a white hooded top with silver spots, and Evie is wearing jeans and a purple hooded top.

'He called me a Greench,' Evie replies. We are talking about Liam. 'And then he said I was like Ebenezer Scrooge who hated Christmas, only I should be called Eco-nezer Scrooge.'

'That's quite clever!'

'I thought it was rude.'

'But why was he calling you names?'

'All I said was that perhaps we should do without fairy lights this year in order to save the planet. He totally overreacted. My family can be so difficult. The other day I asked Mum not to use the dishwasher in order to reduce our carbon footprint – and so she made me do all the washing-up!'

'Harsh!' I exclaim. 'But I think you could probably have a few fairy lights. You're not like some people who cover their houses in so many lights that you can see great holes in the ozone layer opening up above their roofs!'

'I suppose so. I'm not a Greench!'

'No – you're not.'

'I like Christmas – I really do. I'm planning to look around for possible gifts today for family and friends.'

'Don't forget that we agreed with Cassia, Ellen and Salma that we wouldn't spend more than three pounds on presents for each other – and they want to come with us on a Secret Santa Christmas shopping spree in a couple of weeks' time.'

'That should be fun! Especially if we've managed to save Samson by then – we can celebrate!'

'Do you really think Meltonio will change his mind about eating him?'

'I hope so. I just don't know . . .'

* * *

66

When we reach the shops, we immediately go to our favourite one, which is Evie's mum's shop, Fashion Passion, where we look at the cool new stuff. I love the colourful knitted tops and dresses, and the funky hats and gloves. We chat to her mum's assistant, Gabby, and then wander out to the shopping centre, arm in arm.

'Look!' Evie exclaims, pointing at a shop front painted purple and green. 'There's that new shop that Mum was talking about – let's go in.'

The new shop is called Funky Fairtrade Fare, and it sells gifts, cards and novelties, all ethically-produced.

'This is so cool!' Evie enthuses. She holds up a little red, green and gold ornamental elephant woven from shredded palm leaves from sustainable crops. 'I've got to have it!' she squeals. 'Look at all these lovely shiny things. Come along, Lola – embrace your inner magpie!'

'Er – Evie . . .' I say, tentatively. 'Perhaps we should keep our money for the farmers' market.'

'Oh.' Evie sticks out her bottom lip. 'I suppose you're right,' she says.

I drag her unwillingly out of the shop before I succumb to the temptation to buy myself some colourful beaded hairbands. I sometimes think that my mousey-brown hair needs brightening up!

Before we make it to the farmers' market, we are

irresistibly drawn into another of our favourite shops, Bodyzone, attracted by the enticing and heady smells. I have to stop Evie from splashing our cash on a bright green Geo Phyzz Ballistic Bath Bomb and some Squeaky Green Passion Fruit and Papaya Shampoo and Conditioner.

'I'm going to get this for Liam for Christmas,' Evie announces, holding up a product called Greenbody Deodorant Powder. 'It contains natural ingredients, unlike Liam's Bodyblitz Bodyspray. I dread to think what chemicals that has in it. It would be great to get him to use this instead! He could even sprinkle some in his trainers to combat the awful pong.'

I sniff the Greenbody deodorant. It smells pleasantly of fir trees, although I really like the smell of Liam's usual bodyspray, despite the chemicals it contains, and those produced as it is made.

By the time we get to the farmers' market, the sky has clouded over and gusts of cold December wind are lifting and rustling the green-and-white awnings over the twenty stalls which make up the Shrubberylands farmers' market. We join the crowds of people milling around the marketplace, looking at the freshly dug and cut vegetables and salads, homemade chutney, fudge and tempting cakes.

'Oh!' Evie stops suddenly in her tracks in front of a stall with a sign saying: *Venn Farm Organic Pork Products and Organic Rescue Chickens.* 'This must be the farm where Samson was born! This is where he came from!'

A large, friendly-looking man in a green apron and a straw hat with a green ribbon round it, standing behind the stall, says, 'Can I help you two young ladies? All our products are guaranteed free-range and organic – today we have our special sausages made with organic herbs, pork loin, pork chops, pork medallions, pork, pork, pork, pork, pork . . .'

This is not actually what he says, but it sounds like it to us.

' . . . pork, pork, more pork, our home-cured honey-roast ham, back bacon, and pork burgers.'

'Do you kill all your pigs?' Evie asks abruptly.

The large man looks taken aback. But he quickly recovers and answers Evie's question.

'No, we keep some of them for breeding.'

'How do you choose the ones you keep for breeding?'

'We choose the healthiest, most robust pigs: bright eyes, good teeth, tight curly tail, bold and friendly personality.'

'We know a pig like that. I think he came from your farm. His name's Samson, and our friend Meltonio is going to eat him at Christmas. But we don't want him to be killed. Samson's an amazing pig. Can you help us to save him?'

The large man looks thoughtful. 'I'm very sorry,' he

says. 'But I can't really help. I sold Samson to Meltonio, and what he does with him is his own business. I will be assisting with the slaughter.'

Evie looks sick, and I feel as though I can't swallow properly.

'But if there was a lady pig – a sow, I mean – couldn't Samson be kept for breeding?' Evie asks.

'In theory, yes. But that's up to Meltonio.'

'Do you have any sows which Samson could breed with?' I launch in.

'No – I have the right number of breeding boars and sows at the moment. I'm sorry – I have to serve the next customer now. Give my regards to Meltonio.'

Evie and I have to move aside as a determined-looking woman with a large fabric bag stocks up with enough pork to feed a hungry football team.

'That's it!' Evie exclaims. 'We need to persuade Meltonio to keep Samson for breeding purposes!'

'But that means he'd need to get a sow as well.'

'Yes! We could help to find Samson a wife! There must be dating agencies for pigs.'

I can't help giggling. 'Perhaps we should concentrate on sourcing our ingredients,' I suggest. 'But we'll certainly look into the whole pig marriage thing.'

As we wander away, arm in arm, I ask, 'What are rescue chickens?'

'I think they're battery hens like the ones at

Reginald Rooster's, and they get rescued and restored to health.'

'That's good. So the people at Venn Farm must be nice if they have rescue chickens.'

'I suppose so.'

We pass an organic egg stall, which proudly proclaims that it is the winner of the Compassion in Farming Good Egg Award. Then we spend a long time standing at the Fairtrade organic chocolate stall, gazing at all the different kinds of chocolate with longing in our hearts.

'I want it all,' I say, finally.

'Fairtrade chocolate is the only chocolate guaranteed to be produced without child slave labour,' says Evie. Somehow her statement seems more respectable than mine.

We buy several bars of dark chocolate for cooking with, and another bar for sitting in our rooms listening to the latest chart hit by Boys Next Door whilst painting our toenails with.

'We'd better not spend all our money here,' I say, dragging myself and Evie unwillingly away. 'We need carrots and other stuff.'

We stop at the jam and preserve stall where we buy a jar of organic mincemeat.

'Mince pies ought to be popular at this time of year,' I say.

'I certainly hope so,' says Evie. 'That jar cost loads.'

'We could make wholemeal pastry for the mince pies, to make them healthier,' I suggest.

I manage – just – to persuade Evie that it is a good idea to buy a bag of organic pitted prunes.

'They're a healthy snack,' I say. 'Mum's always eating them.'

'Are you intending to cure the whole school of constipation?' Evie inquires. 'Because it certainly seems like it.'

We only have a few coins left – enough for some freshly-dug earth-covered carrots and a few organic apples, leaving just enough money for us to share a hot chocolate at Luigi's, where I have persuaded Evie that we should go next, as it is beginning to rain and we are both feeling cold.

As we walk up the high street towards Luigi's, a Reginald Rooster delivery van passes by and heads up the road in the direction we are going. Evie makes a warding-off-vampires sign at it, and then gasps, 'Oh!'

'What is it?'

'It's stopping outside Luigi's! It's making a delivery! Oh – yuck! Luigi uses Reginald Rooster stuff! I don't want to go there any more.' She turns and heads back the other way. I run after her and grab her arm.

'Evie! Please! We're only going to have a hot chocolate!' And see Liam in his waiter's uniform.

'What harm is there in that? We could even ask Liam to persuade Luigi not to use Reginald Rooster stuff in the future!'

'Liam? But he thinks Reginald Rooster products are great.'

'But it's worth a try, isn't it?'

'Oh – I suppose so . . .'

The lure of getting out of the rain and having a steaming mug of hot chocolate is what finally persuades Evie that we should still go to Luigi's.

It is warm and cosy inside Luigi's café/bistro. There are red-and-white checked cloths on the tables, some of which are set back into alcoves, and bunches of garlic and pimentos hang from the ceiling over the bar and service area, behind which stands Meltonio, resplendent in a huge green apron over a white shirt, black bow tie and black trousers, serving coffees and other drinks. Jazz music is playing gently in the background, and there are customers at most of the tables, eating, drinking and chatting. We recognise some of them as Sixth-Formers from our school.

'I've been here once with Mum,' says Evie. 'We sat at that table over there. Look – it's free. Let's grab it!'

I am scanning the café for a sighting of Liam.

'Oh – there he is! There's your brother!' I exclaim, excitedly, pointing. 'Hi, Liam!'

'Sit down and stop pointing!' Evie hisses at me. 'Do you really want Liam to kill me?'

I wave to Meltonio instead. He waves back.

Liam looks very smart in black trousers, shiny black shoes, a white shirt and a short green apron. He is not wearing a bow tie, but otherwise it all seems very similar to my dream. I just hope the café doesn't catch fire like it did in my dream. I glance around nervously for giant frogs.

Liam comes over to take our order.

'OK, you two,' he says. 'Make your order, have it and then get out of here.'

'Is that how you talk to all the customers?' Evie inquires, and I start giggling.

'I'm asking you nicely not to embarrass me,' Liam says.

'*Would* I?' says Evie, all innocently. 'As if.'

'OK – that's enough. What do you want?'

'I want you to tell Luigi to stop using Reginald Rooster stuff in his kitchen.'

'Does he?'

'Er – *hello*? We just saw the delivery van stop right outside, about five minutes ago.'

Liam shrugs. 'I'm just a waiter. What goes on in the kitchen is nothing to do with me.'

'But it's awful, Liam! Wait till you see the conditions those chickens are kept in – it's so wrong! But people keep buying the chicken because it's cheap. If everyone stopped buying it, Reginald Rooster would go out of business and that would be a good thing.'

Liam shrugs. 'Luigi has a business to run, I suppose. He has to buy his chicken cheaply in order to make a profit. I can't tell him how to run his business. If I did, he'd probably sack me – and I need this job in order to save up for college. Can you hurry up and order, please? There are other customers waiting.'

'We'd like a hot chocolate, please,' I say, as Evie has slumped down in her seat, arms folded and a face like thunder, refusing to talk to Liam.

'Just the one?'

'Yes. We can only afford one,' I say, grinning apologetically while Evie glowers at me across the table.

Rather than looking at Evie, I glance around the room, observing the framed photographs on the walls. Many of them are portrait shots of men with curly black moustaches.

'They must be relatives and ancestors of Meltonio and Luigi,' I remark.

Evie is still looking sulky. The smell of rich sauce and pasta and other appetising dishes is wafting around the café as the waiters ferry dishes to the tables, and my mouth begins to water. Oh no! What if Evie notices?

She is inspecting the menu. 'There are lots of

dishes with chicken in them,' she says. 'How awful! I would rather die than eat any of it, knowing how they treat those wretched chickens! How about you, Lola?'

'Oh – definitely! You're absolutely right! I certainly wouldn't have any of the chicken dishes – even if I wasn't a vegetarian,' I add, hastily. 'Which I definitely am . . . of course . . .' My voice trails away as a particularly appetising bowl of spaghetti bolognese passes by. I quickly look up at the ceiling and pretend to be thinking of other things.

'Shall I go and talk to Meltonio?' Evie asks. 'I could persuade him to talk to Luigi about the chicken – and I could have a word with him about finding a mate for Samson and keeping him alive for breeding purposes.'

'Er – no, Evie. It looks like Meltonio's really busy at the moment. Don't you think it would be better to wait until we see him tomorrow? It would be much easier to talk to him then – and we can show him the chicken film, which will help to make sense of what you're saying.'

'I suppose you're right. You usually are.'

'Oh – er – not really!' I am still feeling guilty about my secret non-vegetarianism.

'Is that Luigi?' Evie asks. A smaller version of Meltonio has burst briefly out of the kitchen, wearing a chef's hat, fluttering his hands animatedly and shouting something in rapid Italian. Then he disappears back into the kitchen.

'Probably,' I say.

Liam brings us two steaming mugs of hot chocolate, piled high with cream and chocolate shavings.

'Er – we only ordered one,' I say, nervously.

'The other one's from Meltonio,' Liam tells us. 'It's on the house.'

Back at Evie's house we lay our ingredients on the kitchen table. Chocolate, mincemeat, more chocolate, pitted prunes, apples, Meltonio's pumpkin (which I fetched from my house) and two lovely bunches of carrots, one of which is for Evie's mum. Evie rummages in the cupboards and finds a family-size box of branflakes, wholemeal flour and a whole armoury of kitchen utensils, mixing bowls and baking trays. She goes to the fridge and fetches margarine, milk and eggs.

'Urgh! Now that I'm a vegetarian I can't bear seeing dead things in the fridge!' she shudders.

'Dead things?' I query.

'There's a chicken in there,' she says. 'At least it's not one of Reginald Rooster's – it's got that RSPCA Freedom Food Mark. But it's still dead.'

I feel a pang of guilt, knowing that last night I ate a dead thing – and enjoyed it.

'Wouldn't it be worse if you found a live chicken in the fridge?' I suggest.

'Don't be silly, Lola. Right – I think that's everything . . . Let's get cooking!'

Several hours later Evie and I are both slightly red in the face, we both have flour patches all over our clothes, Evie has somehow managed to get organic chocolate in her hair, and we have only fallen out twice.

We fell out first when I was dancercising – which is a cross between dancing and exercising – while listening to the radio and unfortunately bumped into Evie, who dropped a plate of branflake cakes on the floor, so that they had to be composted. Fortunately the plate didn't break.

The second falling-out occurred because I let our first attempt at wholemeal pastry burn because I was busy texting Ellen while Evie was washing carrots and chopping and de-seeding the pumpkin. Evie got cross and had a go at me, saying that my pitted prunes looked like squashed dead bats and would put everyone off coming anywhere near our stall.

Then we made up and made more pastry, successfully this time. Neither of us knew what to do with the pumpkin, until Evie suggested glazing each individual chunk with honey, roasting it in the oven and serving it on cocktail sticks. I tried a piece and was nearly sick. We have not yet decided whether to serve it on our stall.

Standing back, we survey the results of our endeavours. There are two large plates of chocolate branflake cakes and a big pile of organic mince pies which are only slightly burned, the prunes, apples and carrots, and strange pumpkin pieces. 'We're going to need to buy more ingredients if we want to keep our stall going,' says Evie.

We put everything in airtight containers. 'I hope it stays fresh till Monday,' says Evie. 'We'll keep it in the fridge.'

All around us the kitchen is a scene of complete devastation, with dirty bowls and used kitchen utensils strewn in all directions, and smears of butter and flour on all the surfaces and also on the floor.

Evie's mum comes into the kitchen, has a fit and storms out, telling us to clear up the mess at once and make the kitchen spotless before she comes back again.

'I suppose that now is not a good moment to ask your mum for more money for ingredients,' I remark.

Evie's dad is more sympathetic. He helps us to clear up, and says that he is not doing much tomorrow so would we like him to make some things for our stall. He offers to make sundried tomato bread, date and walnut cake, and a carrot cake as well, if we like.

'Oh – thanks, Dad!' Evie hugs him. 'That would be great!'

'You'll probably need a lift to school on Monday,' says Evie's dad. 'I should be able to manage that as well.'

'Your dad's the best,' I say to Evie, after he has gone and the kitchen is clean and tidy again. 'Can I stay with you tonight for a sleepover? We can make marriage plans for Samson!'

For some reason Evie becomes a little cagey and evasive, muttering about being tired and 'homework' and 'having things to do'.

'Oh . . . OK, then,' I say, slightly taken aback and trying not to be offended. 'I'll see you tomorrow, when we go to Meltonio's. I'm thinking of cycling there.'

'Cool – I'll cycle, too. And I expect Liam will bring his bike. He sounded quite keen to meet Samson when I asked him last night.'

'OK – well – I'll see you tomorrow.'

'Yes! See you tomorrow!' Evie hugs me. 'You can text me or email if you want to,' she adds, seeming keen to make it up to me for not having a sleepover.

But it seems strange – I wonder why . . .

I soak my cares away in a long, luxurious Green Green Bath of Foam before retiring to bed. A good wallow definitely helps. The delicious cheese and tomato pasta, which Mum cooked this evening, also helped. I am beginning to enjoy being a vegetarian, and I think

I may be able to manage it full-time instead of part-time. Evie is going to be proud of me – she is so strong and has so much willpower. It's great that we can now be vegetarians together. But I still feel puzzled and slightly hurt that she didn't want me to stay for a sleep-over ...

Eco-info
On average, every person in the UK throws away their own body weight in rubbish every seven weeks.

Chapter Six

'Hurry up, Liam – we want to go and see Samson!'

'OK – don't get your organic free-range cotton knickers in a twist, I'm just coming!'

We are waiting in the hallway at Evie's house, and Evie is fastening her cycle helmet. Her flame-red curls tumble out from beneath it. 'I'm going to get terrible helmet-hair!' she groans.

'I like your boots!' I exclaim.

'Aren't they cool? They're fake sheepskin and they're really warm. As a vegetarian, of course, I could never wear the remains of a dead sheep on my feet but these are definitely fake. Mum had a few pairs for me to try for size, but she nearly didn't let me because she was in a mood.'

'Why?'

'Because there weren't any branflakes left for her

breakfast this morning – we used them all yesterday. But I let her have a pitted prune. Oh – why is Liam taking so long?'

We can hear him doing things in the kitchen, so we go to have a look.

'Eurgh! What's *that*?' Evie cries in tones of disgust. Liam is mixing some sticky gooey brownish stuff in a bowl.

'I'm being eco-friendly,' he replies.

'How exactly?' his sister asks.

Liam pauses to scrape a dollop of marmalade from a used breakfast plate into his mixture. 'You're always going on about how we shouldn't waste stuff because it all goes to landfill and releases methane, and so we should only buy as much as we need and turn any leftovers into something else so we use it all up. That's what I'm doing.'

'But . . . what is it? What have you put in there? It looks foul, and it smells . . . yuck!' Evie recoils, covering her nose with her hand. 'Oh – gross!'

'I think it's OK,' says Liam, still stirring. 'I used up all the leftover bits of cereal from this morning, and then I threw in half a tin of cold baked beans which I found in the fridge, some Marmite which I was able to scrape from a pot which was about to be thrown away, some marmalade, soggy scraps of toast, half a yogurt – someone, who shall remain nameless, had only eaten half the pot and was going to waste the rest – half a banana, leftover mashed potato, some cold peas and carrots, a squishy tomato or two, cold congealed porridge and a dash of milk. Oh, and some stewed tea, from the bottom of the teapot. And I made it specially for YOU!' He offers Evie a large dollop of the mixture on a spoon.

Evie shrieks and runs round the kitchen table with Liam in pursuit.

'What's the matter?' he cries. 'I thought you didn't like wasting stuff?'

Evie's mum comes into the kitchen and tells them to stop making so much noise. 'Oh!' she exclaims, peering into the bowl of strange mixture. 'What is *that*?'

'It's leftovers,' says Liam. 'It's all the stuff which Evie wastes – every day!'

'It's not just me!' Evie exclaims indignantly.

'But why did you mix it all up?' their mum asks. 'Liam – for goodness' sake! Shouldn't you have grown out of this sort of behaviour by now? I would have thought that working in a café would teach you the importance of not making a horrible mess!'

'Sorry, Mum.' Liam grins sheepishly. I like his grin.

I have a sudden brilliant idea. 'We could take Liam's mixture as a present for Samson!' I suggest.

Evie thinks that this is a great idea and suggests that we also throw in the pumpkin chunks, which have gone brown and strange-looking. We ladle the yucky mixture into a plastic container, which Evie stuffs into her backpack along with the chicken film. 'It had better not leak!' she says.

'You'd better tell Meltonio everything that's in it,' her mum advises, 'in case there's anything not suitable for pigs.'

'We will,' Evie promises. 'I wouldn't be surprised if Samson turned up his snout at Liam's glop anyway, if he's got any sense!'

Liam nearly doesn't come with us, partly because he doesn't want any of his friends to see him going cycling with his sister and her friend, and partly because he is not sure whether he wants to spend his Sunday talking to a pig when he could be watching sport on television. He grumbles that it is cold outside, which is true. Last night, cold settled on the world like a freezing but transparent sheet.

But we manage to persuade him, and soon we are wheeling our bicycles up to Meltonio's door. Evie found cycling up Hill Rise challenging, so she got off and pushed, and I got off and pushed too, to keep her company. I think I need to do more cycling – it is good exercise. Although the day is cold and grey, I feel hot! Liam cycled on ahead of us – he is very fit, despite his dodgy diet of fast food and salty snacks. I think Evie's parents make sure that he eats enough properly nutritious food.

Meltonio welcomes us and takes the plastic container of glop. We tell him what is in it. He says that he will keep it for later – this may be a polite way of saying that he will throw it away in the compost later . . . He tells us that Mrs Meltonio and the children have gone to Luigi's house so that the children can play with their cousins – so the house is unusually quiet.

Liam and Samson immediately bond.

'I thought they would,' says Evie. 'They have a lot in common. They even speak the same language.'

Samson has put his front trotters up on the fence post and is nuzzling against Liam's face with his soft snout while Liam tickles his silky ears. They are both grunting softly to each other.

'What are they saying?' I ask.

'I think Samson's saying how cool it is to meet a fellow pig,' says Evie. 'And Liam's asking if they can roll in the mud together.'

Soon Liam is helping Meltonio to muck out Samson's little house while Evie and I fetch fresh straw from a nearby shed. Liam uses the hose to top up the pig puddle with fresh water, and Samson grunts happily and then rolls in the puddle, splashing us all with droplets of mud. Evie and I squeal and leap out of the way, but Liam stays where he is, admiring his new friend.

We accompany Meltonio as he trundles a wheel-barrow full of pig muck to the compost area.

'Meltonio ...' Evie begins. 'Have you ever thought of finding Samson a wife? You could keep him and breed pigs.'

Meltonio laughs. 'But I already have so many children – why would I want piglets as well? There is not enough room.'

'So you wouldn't even consider it? Samson would make such a great dad!' Evie continues imploringly.

Meltonio sighs. 'I know that you are trying so hard to persuade me not to eat him,' he says. 'You are kind-hearted girls. But the pig is a farm animal – it is natural for people to keep pigs and to use them for meat to feed their families. And what I am doing is better than going to the supermarket and buying pork from pigs which are kept indoors and never see daylight or smell the fresh air until the day they are slaughtered.'

Evie sighs, too. 'But Samson's special!' she insists. 'Everybody loves him!'

Meltonio is humming to himself. I don't think he wants to listen. Perhaps it is time to change the subject from pigs to chickens.

I start by thanking Meltonio for our hot chocolate at Luigi's. Then I mention that we saw a Reginald Rooster delivery van outside.

'Oh yes,' says Meltonio. 'Luigi gets all his chicken

from Reginald Rooster. It is nice and cheap.'

This is Evie's cue to launch into a tirade about the evils of intensive chicken farming, and Reginald Rooster in particular.

Meltonio says that he is sorry to hear about the chickens, but that he doesn't interfere in his brother's business and he has to be loyal to Luigi. So there is nothing he can do.

'I've brought that chicken film I was talking about,' says Evie. 'Please can we show it to you? It might make you see things differently.'

We attempt to drag Liam unwillingly away from Samson. They are now both on all fours, grunting happily over some rotten apples.

'I'll be back soon, pig,' Liam calls to Samson, reluctantly getting up to follow us. 'Keep the sty warm for me!'

'Please take off your shoes and boots,' says Meltonio when we reach the back door. 'And brush off as much mud as you can, or Mrs Meltonio will not be pleased with me.'

He takes us into his study, which is full of photos of his children and some hanging portraits of the moustachioed ancestors. There is a desk covered with papers, a computer, a bookcase stuffed with books, some comfortable sagging old chairs, and a television and DVD player in the corner. There is also a violin case in the corner.

Liam sees me looking at the violin case. 'Careful – it might not be a violin!' he whispers. 'Perhaps Meltonio's in the Mafia – it might be a machine gun!'

'Shh!' I whisper, feeling very embarrassed in case Meltonio overhears.

Evie has seen the violin, too. 'Oh!' she exclaims. 'I play the violin! Do you play the violin, Meltonio?'

'A little,' he replies, smiling. 'Sometimes I play to Samson. It soothes him.'

'Oh – I'd love to hear you play!' Evie exclaims. 'Would you play to Samson while we're here?'

Meltonio chuckles. 'Well, maybe – before you go,' he says. 'But now we must watch your film about chickens.'

Liam flumps down in an old leather armchair. 'I could be watching the rugby,' he grumbles. 'Instead of which I'm watching a chicken DVD!'

'Shh! You should be grateful to your sister, Liam!' Meltonio reprimands him. 'She is educating you, eh?'

Evie smiles a superior smile at Liam, who rolls his eyes, and I start giggling.

But we soon stop smiling as the programme begins and the dreadful scenes in the chicken sheds unfold.

'These are the chickens which Luigi uses in his kitchen,' says Evie. 'These are Reginald Rooster's chickens. This is how they live – if you can call it a life.'

'Oh! It is shocking!' Meltonio exclaims, looking very upset. 'It is wrong to treat living creatures like that! They can feel pain, like you and me. It is wrong – so wrong!' He wipes a tear from his eye with a large red-and-white spotted handkerchief.

'It's horrible,' groans Liam. 'I don't think I want to eat any more Reginald Rooster Golden Nuggets, or any of his other stuff. This film has put me right off.'

'Good!' says Evie with satisfaction.

We watch the rest of the programme, and Meltonio nods his head approvingly and applauds when we come to the bit about healthy organic chickens.

'Bravo!' he cries. 'This is how chickens should live. These chickens look like the ones at Venn Farm, where Samson comes from.'

'The rescue chickens?' I ask.

'That's right! They are very happy hens!'

When the film has finished, Evie asks Meltonio again if he will try to persuade Luigi not to use Reginald Rooster's chickens in his kitchen. This time Meltonio says that he will try, but he doesn't think that Luigi will listen.

'Would Luigi watch the film?' Evie asks.

'I don't think so. He is always too busy, planning menus, cooking, and running his kitchen. And he doesn't like to listen. You don't know Luigi – it is hard to persuade him. But I will try.'

'Thanks, Meltonio!'

Liam gets out of his chair and asks if he can go back to see Samson. Evie and I ask Meltonio to bring his violin.

Samson is trotting round his enclosure when we reach him. He starts grunting excitedly as soon as he sees us and rears up to nuzzle against Liam's cheek, inviting Liam to stroke his ears and pat his broad back and sides.

'You're a cool pig!' says Liam. 'A fantastic pig! A distinguished pig! A handsome pig! A superior pig! A pig of great wisdom and talent!' I wonder what Liam's friends would say if they saw him talking to a pig like this.

Samson grunts approvingly. Evie takes more photos. Meltonio gets out his violin, tucks it under his chins and begins to play. He plays beautifully and we are entranced.

Samson stops grunting, gets down and wanders over to his pig puddle. He lies down beside it and heaves a contented sigh. The music seems to be lulling him to sleep.

Liam watches, fascinated, and Evie and I hug each other. 'It's the cutest thing I've ever seen!' she whispers.

'Me too!' I agree.

'But how can you possibly eat an animal you've played the violin to?' she asks me incredulously, as

Meltonio finishes playing and quietly puts his violin away.

We thank him for letting us visit and see Samson. He tells us that we are welcome to come again. We are all talking in whispers so that we don't disturb Samson . . .

Back at Evie's house, Liam enthuses about Samson.

'But Meltonio's going to eat him for Christmas!' groans Evie. 'Can you believe it?'

'It seems a shame,' Liam concedes.

'A shame!' Evie splutters. 'It's more than a shame! It's awful! We've got to make him change his mind and keep Samson alive!'

Liam looks thoughtful.

'And now that you've seen that programme, how can you possibly go on working at Luigi's, knowing that he uses Reginald Rooster's chickens?' Evie asks her brother. 'You should resign in protest! Or tell the other staff. Organise a mass walk-out – a boycott!' Evie is getting carried away.

'I'm sorry,' says Liam. 'I really need that job – I need the money. Besides, I've got to save up for your Christmas present.'

'Oh – er . . .' This last remark seems to put Evie off her stride temporarily.

'Try not to worry,' says Liam kindly. 'Perhaps

Meltonio will change his mind. You saw how fond he is of Samson. I wouldn't be at all surprised if he can't bring himself to eat him. I'll give you another guitar lesson soon, if you like,' he says to Evie, before disappearing into his room.

Evie's house is full of wonderful baking smells as her dad has been busy making bread and cake.

'Thanks, Dad!' Evie exclaims, giving him a big hug as we admire the date and walnut loaf, the carrot cake and the sundried tomato bread. 'They look amazing!'

Her mum, who is somewhere upstairs, has also donated a bunch of organic bananas to go on our stall. 'That's really nice of her!' says Evie. 'Perhaps she's going organic at last – she usually complains about the cost!'

We sit at the kitchen table and start listing ingredients on little signs to put by the cakes and bread.

'Do you think we should try some of these cakes before we sell them?' Evie asks.

I agree readily as my mouth is watering, and she cuts us both a small slice of carrot cake and date and walnut loaf. We also have a chocolate branflake cake each.

'Yum!' says Evie. 'How much do you think we should sell this stuff for?'

'I don't think we should charge too much in case people get put off and no one buys anything,' I reply.

'But the ingredients are so expensive – we've got to cover our costs. There won't be any money left for the Save Samson Fund.'

'We could start growing our own fruit and veg.'

'Er . . . by tomorrow?' Evie asks.

I suggest that we charge fifty pence per cake and twenty pence per carrot, apple or banana, and hope that people buy *lots*. 'How much should we charge per prune?' I ask, but Evie doesn't appear to be listening.

'I've had an idea,' she exclaims, jumping up from her chair. 'I'll be in my room. Would you finish packing up the cakes, Lola? Thanks.' She doesn't wait for an answer. 'You can come and join me when you've finished.'

I protest slightly, but Evie has already gone. When I have finished the packing and labelling, I follow Evie upstairs and find her in her room, at the computer. She is giggling.

'Come and look at this, Lola! It's Samson's blog!'

'Did you write it?' I ask, giggling too.

'No, Lola – Samson wrote it!' Evie rolls her eyes at me. 'Of course I wrote it. What do you think?'

I perch beside her on the chair at the computer and read Samson's blog.

Oink oink! Hello friends! My name is Samson and I am a pig. I am no ordinary pig, as you can probably tell because I am writing a blog.

Welcome to my world! I live with my owner, who is a wonderful man who feeds me delicious slops and other stuff, looks after me and even plays the violin to me. I know that he loves me and that he will never let any harm come to me. I am a pampered pig, and incredibly handsome, charming and debonair. I am irresistible to lady pigs, and I also like to have lots of human friends as I am intelligent, wise, sociable and gregarious. I am also modest and clean, except when I roll in the mud, which I like to do frequently. Keep reading my blog! Oink oink!

'I love it!' I squeal excitedly, clapping my hands. 'It's a really funny idea – a pig blog! But why did you decide to write it?'

'Liam inspired me – the way he was talking to Samson,' Evie replies. 'And I'm hoping that Meltonio will read it, and that it might help to change his mind about eating Samson.'

'That's a really good idea!' I exclaim. 'Can I help to write the next entry on Samson's blog? It's going to be such fun! Let's show Liam.'

We call Liam into Evie's room and show him the blog. He thinks it is very funny – and he also tells us that we are both completely mad. Then he leaves, making pig noises at us.

'You sound just like Samson!' Evie remarks. 'You're

very good at pig impressions.'

'I know,' says Liam. 'But don't tell anyone – or you're dead.'

'It's OK, Liam,' Evie calls after her brother. 'Your secret's safe with us.' She grins at me.

'We could make a sign telling people to go and read Samson's blog, and stick it next to the Save Samson Fund sign on our stall,' I suggest.

'Good idea,' Evie agrees. 'And we can put some of the photos on my phone with the blog, so that people can see what Samson looks like.'

'Cool!' I enthuse.

Evie's mum calls up the stairs to say that supper is nearly ready.

'Er – come on, Lola!' Evie says, ushering me out of her room. 'We haven't put our bikes away. And you'd better get home in case your supper's ready.'

'What's the hurry?' I ask as we head downstairs. I am not used to Evie almost pushing me out of the front door.

'Oh – no reason,' Evie replies.

But I feel certain that there *is* a reason. Why does Evie keep behaving weirdly . . .?

Eco-info

UK households throw away £250-£400 of potentially edible food every year - that's a third of all food bought! Try to buy only what you need and not to be wasteful with food, and compost anything that can't be eaten - it breaks down much faster than if put in a landfill.

Chapter Seven

'Mum! I can seriously do without this! I'm in a hurry – I've got to go and help Evie load all the stuff for our stall into her dad's car!'

It is Monday morning, and Mum has chosen this moment to add to the stress.

'I want you to apologise to Enid Baggot!' she shouts at me as I check that I have remembered everything. 'She phoned to say that she clearly saw you lean over the wall at the front of her garden and take some of her holly!'

'It was only a few leaves.'

'That's not the point – you shouldn't take things from other people's gardens, especially not Enid Baggot's – you know what she's like. Why did you take it, anyway?'

'For homemade Christmas decorations. I've really

got to go, Mum – I'll apologise later. Love you!'

And I escape! At least Evie's mum gave her bananas. All I got from my mum was hassle. Then I feel guilty because Mum has been cooking delicious vegetarian food from the vegetarian cookery book, especially for me. Last night we had individual cheese soufflés, which were as light as a feather. Dad is being kind too – he gives me a pack of muesli bars for our stall. 'Food for the brain!' he says. Dad and I are friends again.

Evie and I are cradling most of the cakes in boxes on our laps as we travel to school in Evie's dad's Monda Civic Hybrid – or the Clean Green Eco-friendly Machine, as it is also known. The carrots and the fruit nestle on the back seat between us, and the carrot cake is sitting on the passenger seat at the front. Shaheen has texted us to ask if she and Aisha should bring in some food for our stall, and Evie has texted back to say yes please. Liam said he would take his bicycle as usual, as he might not be able to resist eating all the cakes. Evie tells him to come along at breaktime and support our stall, and bring his friends – or else!

We are both feeling strangely nervous. What if no one buys anything? What if people laugh at us? What if everyone hates our food?

'So how's the vegetarianism going?' Evie asks me,

trying to distract our thoughts away from the impending organic food business venture.

'Oh! It's going fine,' I reply. I tell her about the feather-light soufflés. I decide that there is no need to mention my momentary lapse with the roast chicken. I ask Evie what she had for supper last night.

'Oh – er – salad . . .' she says, hesitantly.

'Is that all?' I ask, a little taken aback.

'Er . . . and lasagne,' Evie adds, not looking at me but staring out of the window.

Before I can ask her whether I can come round and try her mum's vegetarian lasagne soon, we pull into the school and my mind quickly becomes focussed on setting up our stall . . .

Mr Keys, the school caretaker, helps us to set up a table in a corner of the main hall. Miss Peabody, the geography teacher, flutters in, says that our cakes look delicious and that we are allowed to store the leftovers in a fridge in the staff common room, although she can't guarantee that the staff won't eat them all! I hope she is joking. I wonder if there will be anything left for tomorrow – or perhaps all of it will be left . . . We put up a sign outside the hall to draw people in. It says: *Get your Freshstuff HERE! Healthy organic stuff and YUMMY CAKES!* and there is an arrow, pointing. Evie hastily adds: *Suitable for vegetarians* underneath.

We also spread out the poster we made about Samson at the front of the table. It tells people that we are selling our food in aid of the Save Samson Fund and invites everyone to read his blog.

'We'll start selling stuff at morning break and, if there's enough left, we'll carry on at lunchtime,' says Evie, optimistically, as the bell goes for morning lessons to begin.

'BLEURGH! Rancid!' exclaims Amelia, fluttering her hands in front of her face as if she is about to pass out. 'Prunes make me want to puke! They look like giant squashed beetles!' All the So Cool Girls yell 'BLEURGH!' in unison. I wish they'd shut up, as this must be giving a very bad impression to anyone thinking of approaching our stall.

'Stop doing that!' yells Evie, unable to stand it any longer. She has to yell to make herself heard above the loud twittering of the So Cool Girls.

Two people who are not put off are Jamie and Oliver.

'Have you got any crisps?' they ask.

'No!' growls Evie, glaring at them.

'Any Pot Noodles?' they persist.

'NO!'

It is not going well.

'Hello! Wow – cool cakes! I'll have two of those chocolate ones,' says a familiar voice, rising above the hubbub. It is Liam – and he has brought a crowd of friends. I have never felt so pleased to see him – and I am usually pleased to see him – and Evie looks relieved, too.

Now that Liam has pronounced our cakes 'cool', other people start drifting towards our stall to find out what's on offer. Everyone is curious about Samson, and Evie gets out her phone and shows a fascinated crowd the pig photos. There are loud exclamations of 'Oh! Cute!' and 'I *love* pigs!' Again, Evie and I tell everyone to read Samson's blog. 'It's the coolest blog there is!'

The So Cool Girls melt away, sneering at us over their shoulders.

'Good riddance,' says Evie. 'They can go and stew in their own non-organic juices.' Encouraged, she starts walking round the hall and just outside into the main courtyard, yelling, 'Are you fed up with filling up with junk food crammed with chemicals and heaving with hydrogenated fats? We can help! Go and buy your fresh stuff from Lola in the hall! Get your natural energy-boost bananas now – and all our other delicious stuff! Hurry! Hurry!'

Amelia, who is hanging round just outside the hall, glares at Evie. 'Are you fed up with food freaks telling you what you can or can't eat?' she screeches. 'Then get your sweets from me!' She brandishes a large bag of jelly sweets. The So Cool Girls and some other people crowd around her.

'I despair!' I say, shaking my head sadly. But our friends and some more people are showing interest in our stall, and the Indian sweets, which Shaheen has brought in, attract more attention than Amelia's sweets. Shaheen says that they are called *jalebi* – they are bright orange, sweet and sticky. I am not sure how healthy they are, but they are certainly delicious. Aisha has brought in some lentil samosas, and Evie and I are grateful for our friends' support.

Lee, who is chewing his way through a mince pie, says that our stall is a good idea as his digestive system is not geared up to the bio-hazards of the school canteen. Shaheen says that it is great to have an alternative range of food as she is a vegetarian, like us. Evie smiles at me, and I grin nervously. Mr Woodsage, who is also a vegetarian, buys a slice of carrot cake, and Miss Peabody tries a slice of sundried tomato bread, and says that it is delicious. Mrs Balderdash bustles up to the stall, goes into raptures over all our tempting cakes, buys a slice of date and walnut loaf, a branflake cake, three mince pies and an organic carrot, and bustles away again, beaming at everyone. We seem to be giving plenty of people 'food for thought'.

I can see people outside the window eating crisps and packaged food, but at least our food has appealed to others.

'All our food is guaranteed organic and free from

additives!' Evie calls out. 'It's really healthy and good for you! And it's locally-produced, which cuts down on food miles and carbon emissions! So make sure you carry on eating healthily and buying locally – and don't forget to recycle your rubbish!'

But no one hears the end of her little speech as the hall has suddenly cleared of people.

Evie sighs. 'Why won't people listen?' she laments.

'Never mind,' I soothe. 'You tried really hard, and we've sold quite a lot.' All the chocolate branflake cakes have gone. 'Now we're going to have to buy more ingredients and make some more!' Half the date and walnut cake has also gone, and so has a third of the carrot cake, some of the mince pies, and one carrot. Not a single prune has been sold.

'I don't think we've made much money,' says Evie in a slightly weary voice. 'In fact, we'll have made a loss by the time we've bought more chocolate and bran-flakes on the way home. How are we ever going to raise any money for the Save Samson Fund?'

'We'll just have to keep trying,' I say encouragingly, putting my arm around her. 'It wasn't a bad start. Liam really helped. Let's put it all away for today and, later on, when we've got the ingredients, we can make loads of choccie cakes for tomorrow, because they're really popular. And let's take a slice of cake for Meltonio – we still need to persuade him to turn vegetarian.'

'We must tell him about Samson's blog, too,' Evie adds, cutting off a small piece of date and walnut cake and eating it.

After school we go into town and enter the fridge-and-freezer-humming world of our local Kwikspend Supermarket – there is no farmers' market today. Evie points out the two for five pounds offer on all Reginald Rooster chickens. 'It's cheaper than dog food!' she exclaims in disgust.

We manage to find Fairtrade dark chocolate and two boxes of branflakes – 'One for Mum,' says Evie – and some recycled paper napkins for serving the cakes on: Evie thinks this is a good eco-idea, although it means that we use up all our money. We buy four bars of chocolate for cooking with and a spare one . . . for eating.

'Eating something will help to keep us warm,' says Evie, snapping off a piece of chocolate and handing it to me. It is very cold outside as we walk along the windswept street. Evie's curls are blowing in all directions and my own hair whips across my face.

'I'm glad we brought our scarves today,' I say, my breath like little puffs of smoke, quickly blown away.

'I'm wearing my woolly hat tomorrow,' says Evie. 'Brrr!'

'Oh – look! There's Meltonio!' I exclaim.

We cross the street to talk to him. He is on his way home from Luigi's. He usually does evening shifts at the café/bistro on weekdays, but today he did an extra lunchtime shift and will be going back later.

'Luigi wants me there more of the time,' he tells us. 'It is good for me to have more work, with Christmas coming.'

We tell him about Samson's blog, and ask him if he minds that we have written a blog about his pig. Meltonio chuckles.

'I do not mind at all,' he says. 'I am looking forward to reading it. Samson will be famous!'

'I've got something for you, Meltonio,' says Evie, rummaging in her bag. She fishes out the slice of carrot cake wrapped in baking parchment. It is slightly squashed.

'My dad made it,' Evie tells Meltonio. 'It's fully organic. Vegetarian food can be really delicious. Wouldn't you like to try being a vegetarian, Meltonio? It's so good for you – and for the planet!'

Meltonio thanks us for the cake, but protests that he already does his bit for the planet and healthy eating, reminding us about his compost heap and allotment, which provides healthy home-grown food for his family with no food miles and zero carbon footprint.

'It does "allot" of good!' he jokes. 'But seriously, I could never give up meat. I'm sorry, girls. But this cake is delicious – *molto bene*!'

Evie sighs. She asks him if he has had a chance to talk to Luigi about not using Reginald Rooster's chicken in his kitchen.

'Couldn't he change his supplier to one which has the RSPCA Freedom Food Mark?' she asks.

Meltonio shakes his head. 'I tried,' he says. 'I tried to talk to Luigi. But he said that being green is a luxury for people with time and money and he needs his prices to be competitive.'

Not wishing to give up, Evie asks if we can go to the café and talk to Luigi now. Meltonio says no and tells us that Luigi doesn't like to be interrupted at work. I ask if we can talk to him at his house. Meltonio informs us that Luigi doesn't like to be disturbed at home.

I come to the conclusion that Luigi is a very difficult man – so different from his brother!

Meltonio says that he has to go home. He asks us if we would like to come with him to see Samson. We are very tempted, but I remind Evie that we have a lot of cooking to do, as well as our homework. We ask if we can visit Samson tomorrow instead, after school, and Meltonio says that we can, and we can bring some more friends to introduce to him, if we would like to.

As we walk home, Evie says that she is determined to make Luigi listen somehow.

'I'm not chickening out!' she says, fiercely.

At Evie's house we make more chocolate branflake cakes and eat some of them. I am beginning to feel that I have been eating too much chocolate, even if it is organic. I suggest to Evie that we go for a run down the road and back, as I am worried that my dream of becoming an Olympic athlete may be swept away by a huge wave of chocolate and cake. Reluctantly, Evie agrees to come with me, and we change into T-shirts and jogging bottoms from our PE bags, which we brought home from school today.

It is freezing outside! Evie moans and complains the whole way, and even I am relieved to get back to her house again.

Upstairs in her room, clutching hot-water bottles and wearing fluffy yak's wool socks and woollen hats, with two steaming mugs of hot chocolate to warm us up – this is necessary chocolate! – we write the second instalment of Samson's blog on Evie's computer. It is fun, writing it together, and we can't stop giggling.

Oink oink! Hello, friends, and welcome to the pigtastic world of Samson the Wonderpig! Did you know that pigs are sensitive creatures and we make loyal friends, forming strong bonds with people who treat us well?

All we ask is a plentiful supply of food and to be free to smell the fresh air, feel the sun on our backs and the grass under our trotters – these are basic pig rights! I am a fortunate pig – I have a very kind owner who brings me all kinds of treats. He has also built me a very fine house. But sometimes I dream of love, and one day I would like to settle down with a beautiful lady pig and raise hundreds of children. Now I am going to have a quick roll in the mud and then forage for delectable roots. It's a pig's life!

Oink oink! Bye for now!

Evie and I are both flushed with excitement and pride in our creative outpouring, and we are also breathless with laughter.

'It's the best blog ever!' I gasp. 'I hope loads of people read it. I hope Meltonio reads it – it might tug at his heartstrings and make him decide to keep Samson alive.'

'I certainly hope so,' Evie agrees. 'It really does sound like Samson talking, doesn't it? It's exactly the way he would talk – or write – if he could.'

She calls Liam into the room to look at the blog. He reads it, and grins. 'Next time you should put in Samson's full name,' he says.

'What's that?' Evie asks.

'Handsome Samson, of course!' Liam replies.

'Very good!' I tell him. 'I like that!'

'Just don't tell anyone it was my idea – OK?' says

Liam. 'My friends are already teasing me about having a sister who thinks she's a pig.'

'The cheek of it!' Evie exclaims. But she doesn't look too upset.

Liam leaves again. Turning away from the computer, I sprawl on Evie's bed and browse through the Green Gift Guide which came free with *Green Teen* magazine, the fortnightly must-have magazine for greenagers.

'You can get an umbrella made from recycled plastic bottles,' I read out. 'And there's a silver evening bag made from ring pulls. I might get that for Mum.'

'Do you think she'd like it?'

'I'm not sure . . . She might prefer an orange tree from one of those websites that deliver them to your door. It would be difficult to wrap, though. I'm going to make my own wrapping paper.'

'What from?' Evie asks.

'I don't know – probably the pages of this magazine.'

The bedroom door opens, and Evie's mum looks in. She makes a tutting sound and says that the room is like a pig sty. It is averagely untidy, with a jumble of books, clothes, magazines and chocolate wrappers littering the floor.

Evie retorts that her room is not like a pig sty, pointing out that pigs left to themselves are extremely clean and intelligent animals. It is only some horrible farmers who make them dirty by keeping them indoors in filthy conditions and not allowing them to lead natural lives.

Her mum replies that in future everyone will leave Evie to herself, and then they will see how clean and intelligent she is.

'I wash my hands of your bedroom – and that is flat and final!' her mum exclaims.

'Mum – if I tidy my room, can I have some money to buy more ingredients for our stall? Otherwise we're never going to make a profit.'

'We'll see,' says her mum, leaving the room.

I immediately start tidying. 'Aren't you going to help?' I ask.

'Mum winds me up,' Evie replies. 'So I'm watching my fish in order to de-stress. I'll help you in a moment . . .'

Eco-info
Forty thousand trees are felled each year to make eight thousand tonnes of wrapping paper – enough to gift-wrap Guernsey. Recycled wrapping paper or pages from a magazine puts a nice finishing touch to any eco-gift. Remember to recycle wrapping paper too.

Chapter Eight

I am feeling slightly annoyed with Evie. I did most of the tidying in her room yesterday while she goggled at fish. Then, when her mum called her to have her tea, she ushered me down the stairs and out of the front door at high speed, muttering about being very tired and having lots of homework. But we usually do our homework together!

Today she seems fine again, chatting away happily as we carry our boxes of branflake cakes out to the car. Evie's dad is giving us a lift again, and he has also baked some wholemeal scones for our stall. He even offers to provide us with different kinds of freshly-baked bread every other day, and suggests that we ask the school if vegetable samosas would be allowed. Aisha's lentil samosas were popular, and no one told us we weren't allowed to have them on our stall, so I assume the answer would be yes. I have always known that Evie's dad is an enthusiastic chef, and I am thrilled that he is being so supportive of our stall. Mum, despite her new interest in vegetarian cooking, is still complaining about the cost every time I give her a shopping list of healthy, organic ingredients! So it seems unlikely that we are going to raise any money for the Save Samson Fund, and our plans to buy an island paradise and build an eco-resort on it may have to be put on hold . . .

At morning break I feel more encouraged, as business is brisk. We have replaced the unloved prunes with a big bowl of roasted pine nuts and seeds which Evie found in a cupboard – and I have donated some of the nuts that I usually give to the birds. This causes some of the boys to start flapping and going 'tweet' – they are so immature! But other people really like the seeds and nuts. Mr Woodsage is in favour of vegetable samosas, and promises to put in a word for us with Mrs Balderdash.

Once again, the chocolate branflake cakes are the star of the show. There is now a Christmas tree and decorations in the school hall, so there is a festive feel to our surroundings, encouraging people to eat organic and be merry! More people than yesterday are enjoying the mince pies.

'Don't the decorations look lovely?' Evie exclaims. 'I hope the school remembers to recycle the tree.'

Amelia and the So Cool Girls waltz up to the stall to go 'BLEURGH!' as usual.

'You should try some healthy food, Amelia,' I say. 'It might get rid of your bad attitude.'

Amelia shrugs, curls her top lip and turns her willowy back on us, tossing her long blond mane.

Evie and I grin at each other.

A group of girls crowd around us, clamouring to see the photos of Samson again, and several people tell us that they have read the pig blog. Their friends look interested, and soon everyone around us is talking about Samson and his blog. With a slight feeling of alarm, I hear Evie inviting all of them to come with us to meet Samson after school. There must be nearly twenty people by now.

'Meltonio won't mind – he said we could invite some people,' says Evie, airily. 'And some of them won't come, anyway . . .'

She is wrong. We are joined at the school gates by a throng of at least twenty people, and I feel as if we are leading an expedition as we make our way to Meltonio's house. Fortunately the cold wind has dropped and there is a break in the clouds allowing some weak sunshine to filter through, although it will not be long before it is dark. The low winter sun is fading fast.

'Come along, everyone!' Evie shouts. 'We'd better

hurry if you want to see Samson while there's still light.'

If Meltonio is overwhelmed to see such a large crowd of visitors, he doesn't show it. Beaming happily at everyone, he shepherds them along the path by the side of the house and down the garden to the pig enclosure. Looking back, I see an assortment of mini-Meltonios with their faces pressed to the windows at the back of the house, watching us. Two of the older boys and a girl aged about seven or eight with red ribbons in her dark hair run out to join us.

While people take it in turns to move to the front to get close enough to pat Samson, who seems to be thoroughly enjoying the attention, Evie asks Meltonio if he has seen the pig blog.

Meltonio laughs uproariously, his moustache shaking like Santa Claus's stomach. 'It is – how do you say – a hoot!' he exclaims. 'Or perhaps it is an oink! I told Luigi about it. He is going to read it, too.'

I notice a strange expression float briefly across Evie's face. She purses her lips slightly and appears to be thinking hard.

'What is it?' I whisper to her.

'I'll tell you later,' she replies.

'So what's your idea?' I ask Evie as we roll up our sleeves and get to work churning out more chocolate cakes in her kitchen. Her mum has bought us more ingredients because we – or rather, I – tidied Evie's room so beautifully.

We are listening to Dave Groover's Drivetime Show on the radio while we work. Evie licks some cake mixture off her finger and says, 'We need to turn Samson into a celebrity.'

'A celebrity?' I query.

'Yes. More and more people are hearing about him because of our blog. But that's just at school. We need people in the community to hear about him and read his blog.

'Er – why?'

Evie looks exasperated, as if I am being very slow to catch on. 'Because,' she explains, 'Meltonio couldn't possibly eat a celebrity, could he? No one eats celebrities.'

I can't help giggling. 'I suppose you're right. But how exactly are we going to turn Samson into a celebrity?'

'A photoshoot would be good – with a top fashion magazine or a celebrity gossip magazine. They could do a full colour photo article about Samson showing them around his beautiful sty. Or . . .' Evie notices the sceptical expression on my face. '. . . or we could ask the *Shrubberylands Sentinel* to do an article about him.' Evie's mum's friend, Wanda, is a journalist working for the local paper, and she has helped us in the past. 'But first,' says Evie, 'I have another idea to get Samson some publicity.' She goes over to the phone.

'What are you doing?' I ask.

'I'm phoning the Dave Groover Show.'

'Evie – no! Why? You're mad, Evie!' I am giggling too much to get my words out properly.

'Don't make me laugh, Lola! It'll spoil everything. Dave Groover's always asking people to phone in if they have something interesting or funny to tell people.'

'I wondered why you were jotting down a phone number on the back of your hand just now!' I exclaim. 'It's Dave Groover's number! Oh, Evie! You can't! You —'

'Shh!' Evie flaps her spare hand at me to be quiet. She has the receiver tightly pressed to her ear with the other hand. 'Hello?' she says in a slightly squeaky voice. 'Is that Dave Groover?'

I cup my hand over my mouth and hold my breath.

'Oh . . . right . . . I see,' says Evie.

What is going on? I get up and hover near Evie and the phone, doing a sort of agitated dance.

'I see . . .' Evie continues. 'So you'll put me through to Dave Groover if you think everyone will be interested in what I have to say? Yes – I understand.' Evie gestures at me to be still. 'It's a blogging pig,' she says. 'A blogging pig,' she repeats. 'Er – a pig who writes a blog . . . Yes . . . No – it's a real pig . . . He really exists

'... His name's Samson ... I write a blog with my friend ... My name's Evie ... The blog's really popular ... OK, I'll hang on ...'

'What going on?' I hiss.

'They're having a word with Dave Groover ... Hello? Yes – I'm still here. OK! Yes – I'm ready!'

Evie suddenly looks really nervous, and I emit a high-pitched squeak as we hear Dave Groover's voice on the radio announce: 'And that was the new single by the Sugarplums! And how do we follow that, I hear you ask? Well – how about a blogging pig? That's right! It's a pig called Samson who writes a blog about his life as a pig. It's a pig's life! So I'm going to have a word with a friend of Samson's called Evie and find out a bit more about this amazing pig. Evie ... Evie? Are you there, Evie?'

'Yes,' Evie squeaks. She looks petrified.

'Could you turn your radio down a bit, Evie? There's a bit of an echo.'

I rush to turn the radio down, but I stay with my ear pressed to it so that I can hear.

'And how long has Samson been writing this blog, Evie?' Dave Groover asks.

'Er ... er ... He started writing it recently and ... and ... it's really popular, and ... er ...'

'You're so right, Evie! Someone here at Shrubberylands FM has read Samson's blog and they say it's ace! Just log on to Samsonblog dot . . .'

Evie's expression, which has been very worried, visibly brightens.

'And you know what would be brilliant, Evie? If we could have a word with Samson right now, on the radio. Live! Wouldn't that be great, Evie? Evie? Are you still there? Is Samson there? Just a few grunts, that's all we need.'

Evie's happier expression has disappeared. She looks stricken. At this moment Liam wanders into the kitchen. Evie thrusts the receiver at him.

'Grunt like a pig!' she hisses.

I can see that Liam is about to refuse, so I leap in front of him, imploring him with my eyes. I have never done 'imploring eyes' before – at least not to Liam – and there is a distinct possibility that I just look completely insane.

But to my surprise he shrugs, rolls his eyes and does a quick, 'Oink, oink!' down the phone. He sounds just like Samson. Dave Groover sounds very impressed.

'Brilliant!' he exclaims. 'Totally brilliant! Can you do a few more grunts? That would be pigtastic!'

Liam mouths 'What?!' at us, startled by the radio talking to him.

Evie mouths, 'Go on!' back at him.

Liam grunts into the receiver again.

119

'Thank you, Samson! It's been great talking to you!' Dave Groover exclaims. 'Smashing! A blogging pig – who'd have thought it? But I know all our listeners are going to be keen to read your blog, especially now that they've heard you live on the Dave Groover Show! So this next one's for you, Samson! And for Evie! Cheers, mate! Bye for now, Evie!'

Apparently unable to speak – which is unusual – Evie replaces the receiver, her hand trembling.

Dave Groover plays a song called 'The Funky Chicken'. I decide not to turn up the volume on the radio for the time being.

Liam flumps down in a kitchen chair and directs a hard stare at his sister.

'I'm not even going to ask,' he says, 'what all that was about. All I know is that I am probably going to have to kill you. Everyone is now going to think of me as the voice of Samson the blogging pig.'

'But . . . but they won't know it was you,' says Evie, beseechingly.

'Oh, yeah? Unfortunately I happen to be related to you, Evie. So of course no one will make the connection,' says Liam sarcastically.

'I can tell them that it was an uncle of ours who . . . who does animal impressions,' says Evie, desperately.

'Whatever,' says Liam, disconsolately. 'I don't really want to know. I like Samson – but please don't involve me in your ever-increasing weirdness.' He goes to the fridge, fetches a jumbo sausage roll and a carton of fruit smoothie, and leaves without another word.

'How can he possibly eat sausage rolls?' I exclaim. 'They just make me think of poor Samson. I'm really glad I'm a vegetarian now – aren't you, Evie?'

'Er, yes.' Evie doesn't look at me. She seems distracted, probably because of what just happened on the radio.

'Don't worry!' I say, cheerily, putting my arm round her. 'Liam will get over it. And I think you probably succeeded in turning Samson into a local celebrity! Why don't we contact Wanda next? I like the idea of getting Samson's picture in the papers. But we really ought to get Meltonio's permission, of course. It's a bit late to ask him about the Dave Groover Show – but I expect he'll understand. It was a real spur-of-the-moment thing. But it was a good idea, Evie. You're so funny – it would never have occurred to me to do that!'

Evie looks happy now.

'Oh, and I really don't mind that you forgot to mention my name when you were talking to Dave Groover,' I say, airily. I have decided to be big about this.

But Evie doesn't seem to be listening.

'I've got another idea,' she says.

Chapter Nine

Evie has come round to my house to apologise for ushering me out of her house rather sharply – once again! – as soon as her mum got home from work earlier this evening, just after her interview on the Dave Groover Show.

'I was a bit wound up,' she says. 'I just needed time to recover, that's all.'

'If you say so.' I feel puzzled and slightly upset, as I am usually the one who calms Evie down. So why would she want to get rid of me?

'Shall I tell you about my new idea?' Evie asks, obviously keen to change the subject.

'OK, go on.'

'Meltonio said that he's going to show the blog to Luigi,' says Evie.

'Yes . . .'

'So – I thought that we could write something in Samson's blog about intensive chicken farming. We could make it sound like Samson is talking about how he hates cruelty to all animals, including chickens. We could mention Reginald Rooster. It would be a way of getting our message across to Luigi without interrupting him at work, or disturbing him at home.'

'Hmm . . . But it might upset Luigi – he might think you're having a go at him about using Reginald Rooster chicken in his restaurant . . .'

'That's exactly what I *would* be doing!' Evie exclaims.

'Yes – but maybe having a go at someone isn't the best way to persuade them. Luigi might get so angry that it will make things difficult for Liam because he works for Luigi and he's also your brother. Perhaps you should ask Liam what he thinks.'

'Liam doesn't want to know,' Evie replies stubbornly. 'I'm not telling him.'

'Evie!' I am shocked. 'We can't drop Liam in it like this – it's not right!'

'It's not right to keep forty thousand chickens stuffed together in a shed with no natural light until they die in agony or get slaughtered!' Evie explodes. 'Liam will understand that we had to do it. It's the only way to get through to Luigi. And it will all be worth it when Luigi changes his supplier from Reginald Rooster to a nice free-range, organic chicken farm!'

I swallow nervously. I feel very uneasy. 'You're really going to do this, aren't you?' I ask.

'Yes,' says Evie, firmly.

'I don't really want to be part of it,' I say, awkwardly.

'So you don't care about the chickens,' says Evie in a low voice.

'Of course I do. But I don't want to cause trouble for Luigi or for Liam – or for ourselves. We could get sued by Reginald Rooster.' I am only half serious about this last bit, but Evie doesn't smile.

'I'd better go,' she says, still in a low voice. 'I'll see you tomorrow.' She doesn't look at me as she leaves.

I switch on all the fairy lights in my room. Then I switch them all off again, throw myself on my bed and burst into tears.

I hate it so much when Evie and I fall out. Should I have been more loyal and supportive, and agreed to do what she suggested? Am I a horrible friend? But I really like Liam, and I hate the idea of doing something behind his back, which might cause problems for him. He might hate me for ever! I couldn't bear it! But if Evie hates me for ever then I won't be seeing much of Liam in the future ... Oh, why is life so difficult?

I don't feel very hungry and sit at the table playing with the vegetarian lasagne which Mum serves for supper, pushing it around my plate with my fork.

Mum asks me what's wrong. I reply that nothing is wrong.

'That means that something *is* wrong!' Dad says brightly. 'I'm getting quite good at female psychology!'

Mum glares at him, and he concentrates on his lasagne.

I don't really want to talk about my falling-out with Evie so I excuse myself and go and sit in my room at the computer which has recently been installed for the purposes of homework, downloading music on to my iPod, and emailing my friends, though not necessarily in that order.

With a sinking feeling of trepidation, I look at Samson's blog – there is a new entry. Evie must have written it as soon as she got home.

Oink oink! Hi everyone! It's your friendly neighbourhood blogging pig wishing you all many happy hours of rolling in the mud. Did you know that in summer we pigs roll in the mud to protect our skin from sunburn and keep cool in the sun? So why do we roll in the mud in winter? For fun, of course! Pigs are fun-loving creatures. I must go because I can see my owner bringing a big bucket of steaming swill – YUM! He is such a kind man. Happy guzzling, everyone!
Oink oink!

* * *

Phew! There isn't a single reference to chickens, intensive or otherwise. Perhaps Evie has changed her mind . . . perhaps my reluctance had an effect on her and made her think twice about her idea to mention intensive chicken farming.

Feeling very relieved and much happier, I send a text to Evie saying, *Soz about earlier. Hope u OK. C U 2morrow. XXXXXX*

I switch on my fairy lights again and settle down to make a Christmas list. I wonder what I'll get. But I'd really like some gym equipment and new clothes. Last year an elderly aunt gave me a pink fairy outfit, complete with wings – cringe! Evie made me put it on and then she laughed and laughed until she doubled up and rolled on the floor, still laughing . . . I remember when Evie and I were younger, we used to sneak into our parents' rooms and climb up to have a quick peek in the bags of presents on top of the wardrobe – books were flat and hard, clothes were soft when you poked them . . . Ah! Memories!

I am already missing Evie. I go back to the computer in order to email her. But, before I do that, something makes me hesitate and check the pig blog again.

My premonition is right. There is another new entry, and my heart begins to thump uncomfortably as I read it.

Oink oink! Hello again! Yes – it's ME! Handsome Samson! And I've got something important to say. I've already talked to you about pigs' rights, and now I want to talk about chickens' rights.

It is time to put a STOP to evil intensive chicken farming where forty thousand chickens are cooped up in a shed and forced to eat until they are so fat that their legs won't support them. Then they fall over and get horrible burns on their legs, but their legs are cut off after slaughter so you won't know. Doesn't that sound horrible? But you could be eating one of these ill-treated chickens when you buy cheap chicken at the supermarket, or when you eat chicken at some restaurants, including one called Luigi's . . .'

I gasp in horror, clenching my fists until my knuckles turn white. The blog continues:

Luigi's present supplier of chicken is a big intensive chicken farm called Reginald Rooster's Farmfresh Foods. Reginald Rooster is one of the worst offenders in this country, and the chickens he produces have to be transported many miles up and down motor-ways, which produces loads of carbon emissions.

Please don't buy any more Reginald

Rooster chicken. Instead, look for chicken which has the RSPCA Freedom Food Mark, which guarantees that the chicken is reared without cruelty. Organic, free-range chicken is best, even if it costs more. Isn't it worth it to stop the suffering of millions of chickens? Speaking as an eco-pig who cares deeply about the lives of all animals, everywhere, I would like to appeal directly to Luigi, who I know to be a good man at heart, to change his chicken supplier to an organic, free-range one. Help me to help chickens – and pigs – everywhere. Thank you for reading my blog.

Oink oink!

I feel weak and strange. Everyone is bound to think that I was behind this too, aiding and abetting Evie, even though I advised against it. Luigi will be furious! I hope he never sees it, although this is a forlorn hope, as someone is bound to tell him, and I know that Meltonio reads Samson's blog . . . I feel very small and not very brave. Then I feel ashamed. At least Evie has the courage of her convictions. She isn't afraid to make a stand . . .

I send a very short email:

Saw the blog. Hope things work out. Hope you are OK. Are we OK? Let's not fall out. See you tomorrow.

Something tells me that Evie is going to need my support – and I am not going to let her down. I may not agree with what she's done, but I understand why she did it, and eco-worriers stick together! Evie emails me back to say that we are still friends, and everything is going to be fine. I wish I shared her confidence.

Even a long soak in Green Green Bath Foam fails to relax me completely. I have a restless night, sleeping fitfully and dreaming that I am being chased down the street by a giant, very angry rooster, which is somehow even more alarming than the frog . . .

The following morning we are walking to school as usual, as we only have one batch of chocolate branflake cakes to take in and Evie has fitted them into a large plastic container in her bag.

'We'll need to re-stock with some more apples and stuff soon,' says Evie casually, as if nothing has happened, even though I ran up to her and gave her a big hug and told her I hadn't slept all night. She seems very calm. Too calm, I think. 'Those mince pies are getting harder and harder – we should make some more,' she continues.

'Evie!' I exclaim.

'What?'

'Did you tell Liam what you've done?'

'No. Why? What have I done?'

'The PIG BLOG! What else?' I splutter. 'All that stuff about chickens!'

'He hasn't seen it.'

'But —'

'I hid his laptop.'

'You did WHAT?'

'It's in my room, under the bed. I'll give it back to him soon. I just couldn't face —'

'It just gets worse!' I groan. 'You know that he's bound to find out. What if Meltonio and Luigi see it first? What if they really *are* in the Mafia, and Luigi wants revenge, and Meltonio has to help him, out of family loyalty, and —'

'LOLA! Stop! Please . . . shut up.' Suddenly Evie doesn't seem so calm. She looks pale.

I think we both look pale . . .

We are both subdued as we stand behind our stall at morning break, wearing Santa Claus hats in an effort to look festive and fun – but failing. Our friends have been asking us if we are OK.

'I'm fine,' says Evie, as Ellen gives her a big hug. 'It's nothing – honestly.'

'Are you sure? Are you *quite* sure?' Cassia persists, putting a comforting arm around me.

I have a sudden urge to break down and cry on her

shoulder, and tell her that Evie and I are about to be killed by the Mafia or sued by a giant rooster – or, worse still, that Liam will be furious when he finds out what Evie has done, and he will blame me as well, because I am involved in the blog.

My stomach turns over as Liam and his friends enter the hall.

'You look as bad as I feel,' he says. 'I'm having a really bad day – I can't find my laptop anywhere.'

I swallow hard and try to force my features into a sympathetic expression. But I suspect that I just look deranged.

'There's something else that's weird going on,' Liam continues. 'Loads of people I know hang out at Luigi's because it's a cool place to go – but several of them have said they're going to stop going there because of cruelty to chickens. And it seems to be because of something they've read on Samson's blog. It's really beginning to wind me up because I've got people going "Oink! Oink!" at me as well! I could really do without that. I'm seriously not impressed by all this – it's getting out of hand. So I'm looking for an explanation. Lola?'

I feel as if invisible hands are around my throat, throttling me. 'Er . . . er . . . er . . . Would you like a scone?' I start gabbling.

'No, not really,' says Liam. 'I'd like to find out

what's going on. But I'm sure I'll find out soon enough. Why did my sister just run away?' he asks.

Evie has just left the hall in a hurry.

'Er . . . she needed the loo,' I stammer.

'Hmm . . .' says Liam. 'I'll find out what's going on later . . .' He wanders away, steadfastly ignoring Amelia and her gang, who are all making pig noises and giggling like idiots.

'Cheer up!' says Lee, who has come to the stall to buy a branflake cake. 'Christmas is coming, the geese are getting fat!'

'And so are the chickens,' I say, very quietly. 'And Samson . . .'

Samson's fan club ask us if we can all go to visit him after school today, but I tell them that Evie and I have a lot of homework to catch up on, so we are going straight home.

'OK – so why don't we go tomorrow?' Lee asks.

'Maybe,' I reply, forcing a strangled smile. I don't know what is going to happen yet, and I have a strong feeling of foreboding.

Evie comes home with me and asks if she can hide in my room – for ever.

'Don't tell me you're regretting what you've done,' I say.

'Er . . . no . . . of course not,' she replies, folding her

arms defensively and rocking gently to and fro as she perches on the edge of my bed.

I tell her that she really should go home and return Liam's laptop to him. She looks at me aghast, as if I have just asked her to jump into a pool of snapping turtles and assorted dangerous reptiles.

'I know you're right,' she says. 'You usually are – and I probably should have listened to you. Couldn't I just stay here a little longer? No – you *are* right – I should go . . .'

She gets up, slinging her school bag over her shoulder.

'I'll come with you,' I say, bravely. 'I know that you did what you did for the best of eco-worrier reasons. You always do.'

We hug each other, and go to face the music.

'What the hell have you done?' Liam shouts at us the moment we walk through Evie's front door.

He stands facing us in the hallway, his face like thunder. I gulp and edge slightly behind Evie. All my nightmares are coming true – apart from the giant frog bit, obviously. Or the giant rooster. So far . . .

'I've just been sacked by Luigi!' Liam yells at us. 'He phoned to say that there were bad things written on that stupid pig blog and I must have something to do with it. He heard me on the radio. He guessed that it was me grunting like Samson after Meltonio told him that you were my sister. And he says that I have undermined his business, and then he sacked me for disloyalty. Mum found my laptop under your bed, Evie! I read all that stuff about intensive chicken farming, and so I knew instantly that it had to be you because you're always going on about it! How could you? You must have known that I would lose my job! And you, too, Lola!'

I hang my head, unable to look Liam in the eyes.

'Lola had nothing to do with it!' Evie cries. 'She advised me against doing it!'

But Liam isn't listening. He turns his back on us and stomps up to his room and slams the door. We hear him listening to loud, aggressive music by a rap artist called Snoot Dog.

'I'm so SO sorry!' I whimper, even though Liam can't hear me, the tears rolling down my cheeks.

'You didn't do anything, Lola!' Evie exclaims in a mixture of frustration and despair. 'It was *me*! I really need to go and see Luigi – I've got to sort this out!' She is shaking visibly, and I put my hand on her arm to comfort her.

Evie's parents have come into the hallway to find out what is going on.

'Dad!' Evie appeals to her father in an agonised voice. 'Dad, please can you take me to Luigi's – right now? It's really important. Please, Dad!'

Evie's parents want an explanation, and Evie does her best to make them understand that she is desperate to explain to Luigi that it was she who wrote the chicken stuff on the pig blog, and she wants to get Liam his job back.

Her parents look confused, as though they do not quite understand what is going on, but then her dad says, 'OK – I'll take you. I'll go and get the car keys.'

'Can I come with you?' I ask Evie.

'I want you to,' Evie replies, taking my arm. 'I really want you to be with me, Lola. If you don't mind. None of this was your fault.'

'It's OK. That's what eco-worriers do,' I say. 'They stick together, through the good times and the bad.'

I call Mum and Dad to let them know where I'm going – 'We shouldn't be very long, and Evie's dad will bring us straight back' – and then we go and get in the car.

I notice that Luigi's has fewer customers than it had when I came here with Evie. Only a couple of tables are occupied. Oh dear! This is not a good sign – although I have never been here in the evening before. Perhaps – I hope – this is not unusual for a weekday evening. Evie asks her dad to wait for us in the car – she wants to do this herself.

'If you're sure,' he says, hovering at the entrance.

'I'm sure, Dad.'

'OK – well, you know where I am.' He blows her a kiss and leaves.

Meltonio, who is behind the bar as usual, looks worried when he sees us approaching.

'Luigi is not happy this evening,' he says, shaking his head sadly as he shines a glass with a white cloth. 'Not happy at all.'

'I've come to say sorry about the chicken stuff on Samson's blog,' Evie explains. 'I want to apologise to Luigi – and to you. I'm sorry, Meltonio.'

Meltonio blows on the glass and shines it again. 'It would be better if young Liam came to say sorry,' he says. 'It was a foolish thing that he did. I was surprised that he did it.'

'But it wasn't Liam,' Evie says. 'It was me.'

Meltonio stops shining the glass and looks at her seriously, as Luigi bursts out of the double kitchen doors, red-faced and waving his arms around. 'And now they tell me that they have run out of parsley in the kitchen!' he shouts in exasperation. Then he continues in voluble Italian, subjecting poor Meltonio to some sort of angry tirade about – presumably – the lack of parsley in the kitchen.

Then he sees us.

'Aha! Your brother has tried to damage my business!' he exclaims. 'So I have had to sack him! It is a shame, eh? But he should not have written bad things about Luigi!' His black moustache bristles with outrage and indignation. Luigi is shorter than Meltonio, and we can only see him from his shoulders up to his chef's hat over the bar. He is about the same height as I am – I am taller than Evie.

Taking a deep breath, Evie explains that it was she who wrote the blog and not Liam. She tells Luigi that Liam knew nothing about it, and she tells him that I advised her against doing it.

'Sensible girl!' says Luigi, nodding approvingly at me.

My heart is beating fast, but I feel the need to speak up. 'Evie never meant to . . . er . . . hurt you or your business,' I begin, falteringly. 'And I know she's really sorry if that's what has happened. But she cares passionately about the welfare of animals – and so do I – and I agree with her about intensive chicken farming. It's really horrible. We wanted you to use free-range, organic chickens instead of the Reginald Rooster ones. And Evie was looking for a way of getting your attention . . .'

'She certainly did that!' says Luigi, frowning at Evie.

'But none of this is Liam's fault!' wails Evie, who clearly cannot bear being frowned at by Luigi. 'Please – oh, please can he have his job back?' And she bursts into tears.

The few customers seated at their tables have stopped eating and are watching, fascinated.

Overwhelmed by the situation, I start crying, too.

Our tears have an instant effect on Meltonio and Luigi. Their whole attitude changes and they rush round from behind the bar to usher us to a table, where they urge us to sit down and not to cry. Meltonio hurries away and returns with two hot chocolates, piled high with cream, which he places on the table in front of us.

'You must not be sad,' says Luigi in a much gentler voice. 'Your brother can have his job back – of course he can . . .'

'Oh – thank you!' Evie exclaims, beaming through her tears.

'But you must understand that I am worried about my business,' says Luigi gravely. 'Look how few customers I have here this evening.' He gestures around the nearly empty room.

'I understand,' says Evie, nodding. 'I'm really sorry.'

'A lot of my customers during the day are young people who read this blog,' Luigi adds. 'So it is worrying.'

Meltonio looks thoughtful, stroking his chins. 'I might have an idea to make this all better,' he says. 'But I will need to make phone calls tomorrow.'

'Ah! There is your dad,' says Luigi. 'I think he is wondering what has happened to you. They are both fine,' he says to Evie's dad. 'They are drinking hot chocolate.'

'So I see,' says Evie's dad, his eyes twinkling.

It is a far cry from the Mafia-style execution which I had feared.

'I never know what you're going to do next!' Liam says, shaking his head in disbelief.

We are sitting at the kitchen table, telling Liam the good news. 'And the main thing is that you've got your job back!' Evie exclaims triumphantly.

'I'm glad about that,' says Liam. 'I need to go on bringing home the bacon. It's a good job – Luigi's a good employer.'

'Meltonio said that he had an idea to make everything better,' I say, musingly. 'I wonder what that is.'

'You must be hungry,' says Liam. 'You missed supper. Would you like some —?'

'Oh! No! I'm fine! Come on, Lola – let's go!' Evie springs up abruptly from the table and attempts to drag me out of the kitchen.

'What's the hurry?' I object. I want to stay and talk to Liam! What is the matter with Evie?

'But Mum kept a piece of breaded haddock for you, Evie,' Liam says. 'You asked for it this morning – remember? And Mum bought those organic chips in a biodegradable bag, like you asked her to . . .'

'Haddock?' I repeat. 'Fish? I thought you were veggie . . .?'

I look at Evie, and she looks down at her feet, shifting uneasily.

'I'm a vegetarian who eats haddock,' she mutters.

'And sausages,' says Liam. 'And steak . . .'

'Sausages!' I exclaim, almost unable to believe what I am hearing. 'I thought you said you'd never eat another sausage because of Samson!'

'I only had one,' says Evie in a small voice, hanging her head.

'You had three,' Liam corrects her.

'But . . . but . . .' I stutter. 'I thought you were the strongest-willed person I know! I thought I was the weak-willed one – I had roast chicken! But that was ages ago. Since then I've really liked being a vegetarian. What about all those delicious vegetarian dishes you were talking about, like vegetarian lasagne?'

'I like that too,' says Evie. 'But I . . . er . . . missed meat too much. And Liam kept tempting me . . .'

'Don't you dare blame me!' Liam exclaims.

'But why didn't you tell me?' I ask.

'I didn't want you to know. I didn't want you to think badly of me,' Evie confesses. 'It was my idea to become vegetarian – and then you were better at it than I was.'

'So that's why you wanted me to leave every time

you were about to eat,' I say, as the truth suddenly dawns. 'You didn't want me to know that you were stuffing yourself with meat!'

'Er – you're making it sound worse than it is,' Evie objects. 'I'm still a part-time vegetarian.'

There is an awkward pause, but Evie looks so guilty and miserable that I can't bear it any longer. We look at each other, our lips twitch, and then we burst out laughing.

Liam shakes his head sadly. 'You're both idiots,' he says.

We give each other a big, fat hug, and plan a sleep-over for the weekend to celebrate the fact that we are no longer hiding anything from each other.

Eco-info
Buying local, organic or free-range meat for home is good, but also think about where other meat you eat comes from. Ask restaurants and schools to try and get meat from an ethical supplier, and have better vegetarian options. If no one asks, nothing will change.

Chapter Ten

Oink oink! Yes – I'm back! I had to give up my blog for a couple of days because there were some problems that had to be sorted out. But then I had loads of messages from my many fans saying that they were missing hearing from me. I hate to disappoint anyone, so I've decided to get blogging again. So put your trotters together and let's have a big round of applause for Handsome Samson!

I am at Evie's house on Sunday morning when the phone rings. Evie answers it.

'Oh – hello, Wanda. Do you want to speak to Mum? Oh, you heard the interview? Yes . . . yes . . . yes . . . that's right! Yes . . . yes . . . Lola and I write the blog . . . yes . . . Samson belongs to Meltonio. Er, I should think so . . . He should be there this afternoon . . . yes . . . yes . . . yes . . . yes . . . OK . . . I'll find out and then I'll get back to you. Bye!'

'What was all that about?' I ask, almost burning up with curiosity.

Evie explains that Wanda would like to conduct an interview with Samson and Meltonio, and bring along a photographer.

'She wants to do it this afternoon,' Evie says. 'So I said I'd find out if it's possible and let her know.'

Evie phones Meltonio, who says that he would be happy for Wanda to visit him and take photographs of Samson this afternoon, and a time is arranged – three o'clock – when we can all be there. Evie phones Wanda to let her know.

Meltonio beams with pride in the bright winter sunshine as the photographer from the *Shrubberylands Sentinel* snaps away, taking photos of Samson from every angle, and then taking photos of Samson with Meltonio. Liam, who has come along to see Samson, avoids the photographer. He tries to look cool and über-casual, which is difficult with a very excited Samson squealing and grunting and running around his enclosure in the background.

'Can we have a photograph of you playing your violin to the pig?' the photographer asks Meltonio, who rushes indoors to fetch his violin.

'What gave you the idea to write a pig blog?' Wanda asks Evie.

'Lola and I write it together,' Evie replies. 'We want people to realise what a wonderful pig Samson is.' Wanda is jotting things down on her reporter's pad.

'Wanda . . .' I begin. 'Can you help us? We're really worried because Meltonio said he's going to eat Samson for Christmas!'

'Oh dear!' exclaims Wanda. 'I thought he was a family pet.'

'We really want Meltonio to keep Samson alive,' says Evie, urgently. 'Can you persuade him?'

'Oh! Well – I don't know . . .' Wanda looks perturbed.

Meltonio returns with his violin and begins to play a beautiful melody while the photographer crouches to get a good shot of Meltonio in the foreground and Samson in the background.

Samson stops running around, grunts gently and goes to his favourite place by the pig puddle where he lies down flat on his side, letting the music wash over him.

'Oh – how lovely!' says Wanda under her breath. 'Surely no one could bear to part with a pig like that?'

When Meltonio has finished playing, she tells him how beautiful it was, and then she asks, 'Is it true that you are planning to eat Samson for Christmas dinner?'

Everyone, especially Evie and me, holds their breath, waiting for Meltonio's answer.

Meltonio sighs and looks at Samson, who has woken up and is now rolling in his pig puddle.

'No!' he says, firmly. 'It would be like eating my friend – I cannot do it!'

Evie and I whoop with joy and hug each other. Then we hug Meltonio. Then we hug Wanda. Then we try to hug Liam, who runs away, vaults over the pig netting and takes refuge in the pig enclosure with Samson.

'Samson is famous now,' Meltonio continues, waving his hand to indicate the photographer, who is creeping up on Samson and Liam, who are on all fours, grunting at each other. 'He is – how do you say – a celebrity! He will want to eat his swill out of a silver trough!'

Meltonio sounds very proud.

'So what are you going to do with him?' Wanda asks. 'Will you keep him as a pet?'

'No. It would not be right. Pigs are sociable creatures, and I don't want Samson to get lonely. I want him to have a wife!'

'Oh – cool!' Evie and I chorus. Then Evie looks surprised.

'But I thought you said that you didn't have enough room for another pig,' she queries.

'I don't. But I spoke to my friend at Venn Farm, and one of their boars has just died. So there is room for Samson to return there – and they have a lady pig for him. Her name is Delilah! So Samson will be happy. I will miss him, of course. But I can still visit him. We all can.'

Wanda laughs, and Evie and I giggle. 'Samson and Delilah! How lovely!' says Wanda. 'I hope your friend at Venn Farm will let us have a photo of the happy couple for the *Shrubberylands Sentinel*!'

'We really have saved the bacon!' I exclaim happily. Then I remember something. 'Meltonio . . . ?' I venture.

'Yes, Lola?'

'You said that you had an idea to make everything better after all that business with the chickens. What was your idea?'

'Oh – I forgot to tell you! We have all been busy concentrating on Samson. But it is good news – you will be very pleased, I think. Luigi has cancelled his order with Reginald Rooster's Farmfresh Foods . . .'

'Hurrah!' Evie and I cheer loudly.

'Instead, my friend at Venn Farm and Luigi have come to an arrangement. He will supply his free-range, organic chickens to Luigi's restaurant, at a reasonable price, and in return Luigi will mention my friend's farm shop on the menu – so they will help each other's businesses. It is all sorted out, and everyone is happy.'

'And so are the rescue chickens!' I add.

'I'll put something on Samson's blog about Luigi using these chickens in his restaurant,' says Evie, happily. 'Then the customers who got put off by all that stuff about Reginald Rooster and intensive chicken farming should start coming back.'

'That's a really good idea,' I say, and Meltonio agrees.

Samson grunts his approval.

Oink oink! I am a VERY HAPPY PIG! And I am certainly a VIP (Very Important Pig) as well! Because I have a special announcement to make. I am going to get married!

My bride-to-be is the most beautiful sow in the whole wide world, and her name is Delilah. Darling Delilah! Divine Delilah! Delightful delicious delectable Delilah! With the daintiest trotters in the whole world! You are all warmly invited to the porcine wedding of the century! Details will follow. I intend to populate the world with mini-Samsons and mini-Delilahs, and I will let you know about any impending happy events.

Before I trot away, head held high, a spring in my step and an extra curl in my tail, I have some more joyful news to impart. My friend Luigi has decided to serve only free-range, organic chicken at his wonderful restaurant, and I recommend that you all go there soon and enjoy his delicious cooking. *Mamma mia!* It is the best! Bye for now!
Oink oink!
PS Happy Christmas!

* * *

It is the Saturday before Christmas, and both our families have decided to enjoy a celebratory pre-Christmas evening meal together at Luigi's, which has been re-named Samson's. It is much busier tonight than the last time we came here, and all the tables are occupied by happy customers. Liam is our waiter for the evening!

As we arrive, Evie and I excitedly point out two new framed portrait photographs hanging just inside the entrance: one is of Samson, and the other is of another Gloucester Old Spot pig, and underneath it is a label which says *Delilah*. Evie and I used the proceeds from the Save Samson Fund to pay for the newspaper photos of Samson and Delilah to be framed as a Christmas gift for Luigi and Meltonio. Our parents helped us to pay for this, as our fund did not quite cover it – most of the money we earn goes to pay for more ingredients! I don't think we'll ever be able to afford to buy an island in the sun – but we really enjoy running the stall, and it has become very popular.

All the portraits in the restaurant have decorative sprigs of holly on top of the frames – the ones of Samson and Delilah have little bunches of mistletoe over them – and there is a twinkling Christmas tree in a corner of the room.

The article from the *Shrubberylands Sentinel* about

Samson is also framed and hanging on the wall, along with the photographs. The newspaper sent us a set of all the photos, and Liam took the ones of himself and Samson and hid them somewhere, telling Evie on pain of excruciatingly horrible death that she was NEVER to show them to anyone! But I have a feeling that he was secretly pleased with them – he is very fond of Samson.

I am delighted to see that there are several new vegetarian recipes on the menu, and I order a roasted red pepper and houmous wrap with wild rocket salad. Dad orders the curried butternut squash soup. He has shaved off his scraggly beard and looks much better. I am proud of him for being so eco-friendly and travelling by bicycle some of the time – and now it seems as if he shares my preference for vegetarian food!

Hesitantly, Evie asks me if I mind if she orders a chicken and pasta dish.

'Of course not!' I reply. 'I'd much rather that you were honest with me about wanting to eat meat some-times. It's not as if you're a rabid carnivore! And at least we know that all the chicken is free-range and organic.'

I feel very relieved. It is nearly Christmas and everyone is happy. Evie and I sip our organic cranberry and raspberry juice – which also comes from the farm shop, Meltonio tells us – and then we all raise our glasses to Luigi and Meltonio, to Samson and Delilah, and to everyone at our table.

From across the restaurant Meltonio waves to us and calls out, '*Bravissimo!*' We wave back.

Evie beams at me and raises her glass again. 'Here's to us!' she says. 'To eco-worriers!'

'To eco-worriers!' I repeat. 'Triumphant again! We've saved the bacon!'

Eco-info

You can feed seven people with the grain it takes to produce enough beef for one person. If being a total vegetarian isn't appealing, try just swapping one or two meals a week to being meat-free.
It all adds up!

ECO-WORRIERS

Penguin Problems

Committed eco-worriers, Evie and Lola, are very, very concerned about green issues much to the irritation of their gas-guzzling families!

So when they find a penguin chick in the garden they're really worried. Have the ice caps finally melted and the poor penguins been forced into new lands?

It turns out that this particular penguin was taken from the local wildlife park. Could the penguin-napping be linked to the awful, but completely unfounded, rumours circulating about the park? Lola and Evie are determined to investigate further, and the more they find out, the more suspicious they become . . .

ECO-WORRIERS

Tree Trouble

Lola and Evie are very concerned about
the state of the planet and are determined
to get their school to go green.

When they learn about the destruction of
the tropical rainforests, they are even more
concerned. What will happen to all those poor
creatures who live in the trees – let alone
the effect on climate change?

They decide to do their bit to help and
organise a talent show, GreEntertainers,
to raise money for Tree-aid. But first they
need to find some talent . . .

ECO-WORRIERS

Dolphin Disasters

A school trip to a Sealife Centre alerts
committed eco-worriers, Evie and Lola,
to the threat dolphins and other creatures
face from plastic rubbish polluting their
environment. They must do everything
they can to stop it

But raising everyone's awareness is a different
matter and all of their efforts seem destined
to end in disaster - until they come up with
one fantastic idea . . .

For everything Eco-Worriers . . .

www.piccadillypress.co.uk/ecoworriers

Check it out for:

Quizzes

Eco-facts

Downloads

Green ideas

New releases

Ways to get involved

and lots more!

www.piccadillypress.co.uk

☆ The latest news on forthcoming books

☆ Chapter previews

☆ Author biographies

☆ Fun quizzes

☆ Reader reviews

☆ Competitions and fab prizes

☆ Book features and cool downloads

☆ And much, much more . . .

Log on and check it out!

Piccadilly Press